This book belongs to:

....

365
Stories
and
Rhymes

Original stories written by: Catherine Allison, Annie Baker,
Peter Bently, Malachy Doyle, Rachel Elliot, and Timothy Knapman.
Selected stories retold by Cath Ard and Claire Sipi.

Cover illustrated by Júlia Sardà.
Illustrated by: Gabriel Alborozo, Deborah Allwright, Victoria Assanelli,
Barroux, Maria Bogade, Alison Brown, Petra Brown, Julie Clay, Livia Coloji, Charlotte Cooke,
Antoine Corbineau, Ciaran Duffy, Marilyn Faucher, Mar Ferrero, Chiara Fiorentino, Henry Fisher,
Emma Foster, Hannah George, Kim Geyer, Beverley Gooding, Daniel Howarth, Katy Hudson,
Russell Julian, Sean Julian, Dubravka Kolanovic, Emma Levey, Katya Longhi, Polona Lovsin,
Deborah Melmon, Mei Matsuoka, Alessandra Psacharopulo, Kirsten Richards,
Fiona Rose, Loretta Schauer, Gavin Scott, Lisa Sheehan, Christine Tappin,
Erica-Jane Waters, Jenny Wren, Gail Yerrill, and Aleksander Zolotic.

Every effort has been made to acknowledge the contributors to this book.
If we have made any errors, we will be pleased to rectify them in future editions.

This edition published by Parragon Books Ltd in 2016
and distributed by

Parragon Inc.
440 Park Avenue South, 13th Floor
New York, NY 10016
www.parragon.com

ISBN 978-1-4748-2097-4

Printed in China

365
Stories
and
Rhymes

PaRragon

Bath · New York · Cologne · Melbourne · Delhi
Hong Kong · Shenzhen · Singapore

Contents

The Gingerbread Man

There was once a little old woman and a little old man. One morning, the little old woman decided to bake a gingerbread man. She mixed all the ingredients together, rolled out the dough, cut out the gingerbread man, then put him in the oven to bake.

But when the little old woman opened the oven door, the gingerbread man jumped up and ran away.

"Stop!" cried the little old woman.

"We want to eat you!" cried the little old man. And they ran after the gingerbread man. But he was too fast.

"Run, run, as fast as you can. You can't catch me, I'm the gingerbread man!" he sang.

Then he darted into a field, passing a pig, a cow, and a horse. They all wanted to eat him, too!

"I've run away from a little old woman and a little old man, and I can run away from you!" he told the animals. And he sang, "Run, run, as fast as you can. You can't catch me, I'm the gingerbread man!"

The little old woman, the little old man, the pig, the cow, and the horse ran and ran, but none of them could catch the gingerbread man.

After a while, the gingerbread man reached a river.

"How will I get across?" he cried.

A sly fox saw the gingerbread man, and licked his lips.

"Jump onto my back and I will take you across the river," he told the gingerbread man.

So the gingerbread man jumped onto the fox's back and the fox began to swim across the river.

After a while, the fox cried, "You're too heavy for my back. Jump onto my nose." So the gingerbread man scrambled onto his nose.

But as soon as they reached the riverbank, the fox flipped the gingerbread man up into the air and he fell straight into his open jaws. The fox snapped his mouth shut and gobbled him up.

And that was the end of the gingerbread man!

The Bravest Best Friend

Mitch Mouse and Micky Mole were best friends. They played together every day. But one day, Mitch and Micky had an argument.

"Mice aren't as brave as moles," said Micky, puffing out his velvety chest.

"Moles are much more nervous than mice," Mitch replied.

"No they're not!" cried Micky Mole. "You're frightened of loud noises!"

"I'm not!" Mitch Mouse squeaked indignantly. "You're scared of the sunshine!"

"Oh no I'm not," huffed Micky. "I've got an idea. Let's have a bravery competition. Whoever can do the most brave things today is the winner, and the bravest best friend of all time."

Mitch agreed, and set off to prove how brave he was.

First, Mitch went into the jungle. It was dark among the trees. Snakes crossed his path and insects brushed against his fur. Suddenly a troop of screeching monkeys tried to grab him, but Mitch was too quick for them. He dashed into the undergrowth.

"I'm a brave mouse," he told himself. "I'm not scared. I can get through this jungle! If only Micky could see me now!"

At last, Mitch reached a little town on the other side of the jungle. He was tired and hungry, but he kept walking. Then he saw a couple of pampered cats sipping milk and nibbling cubes of cheese.

"Cats eating cheese? Whatever next!" he exclaimed to himself.

His tummy rumbled when he looked at the delicious morsels of cheese. They smelled so good! There was only one thing to do. He had to have the cheese.

Mitch took a deep breath. "I'm a brave mouse!" he muttered. Then he ran out in front of the cats, pulled faces at them, and did a silly dance. They stared at him in amazement. They had never seen a mouse do that before! While they were staring, Mitch darted forward, filled his arms with cheese and ran.

It took the cats a few seconds to believe their eyes. But by the time they realized that a mouse had really just stolen their food, Mitch was long gone.

Mitch raced through the town until he reached the jungle. His legs were aching, but he carried on running. This time he wasn't afraid of the dark. He just wanted to get home so that he could tell Micky all about his amazing day and how brave he'd been.

Exhausted but happy, Mitch finally reached his friend's house.

"Mitch, you'll never guess what I did today!" cried Micky as soon as he saw Mitch, and he told his friend all about his own brave adventures.

"Well, I went to the jungle ..." started Mitch. Then he stopped. Grinning at Micky, he said, "I think we both deserve to win the competition. We're the bravest best friends ever!"

Blow, Wind, Blow

Blow, wind, blow! And go, mill, go!
That the miller may grind his corn;
That the baker may take it,
And into rolls make it,
And send us some hot in the morn.

Sunshine

A sunshiny shower
Won't last half an hour.

Off Together

We're off together. Oh, what fun!
There may be rain or there may be sun.
But we'll all have a lovely time together,
And enjoy ourselves, whatever the weather!

Raindrops

I love to see the raindrops
Splashing on the sidewalk;
I love to see the sunlight
Twinkling in the rain;
I love to see the wind-gusts
Drying up the raindrops;
I love to feel the sunshine
Coming out again!

Rain

Rain, rain,
go to Spain,
Never show
your face again.

Snow

I'm a little snowman short and fat,
Here's my scarf and here's my hat.
When I see the snowfall,
Hear me shout
"All you children please come out!"

How the Bear Lost His Tail

Once upon a time, the bear had a long tail, and the fox was very jealous of it.

"What makes Bear think his tail is so wonderful?" growled the fox, as he looked at his own splendid russet-colored tail. "My tail is much finer than his. I'm going to teach him a lesson."

It was winter, and all the lakes were covered with thick ice. The fox made a hole in the ice and surrounded it with fat, tasty-looking fish. That evening, when the bear passed by, the fox dangled his tail through the hole into the water.

"What are you doing?" the bear asked.

"I am fishing," the fox replied. "Would you like to try?"

The bear loved fish, so he was very eager to try.

"This is what you must do," the crafty fox explained. "Put your lovely long tail in the hole. Soon a fish will grab it, and then you can pull the fish out. In the meantime, you must be very patient and stay perfectly still."

The bear was hungry and wanted to catch some fish, so he did exactly as the fox had told him.

The next morning, the fox went back to the lake and saw that the bear was lying on the ice. He was fast asleep and covered in snow. The hole had frozen over during the night and now the bear's tail was trapped in the ice.

The fox called out, "You've caught a fish! Quick! Pull out your tail!"

The bear woke up with a start and tugged his tail as hard as he could. All of a sudden, there was a loud CRACK! as the bear's frozen tail snapped off.

And that explains why bears now have very short tails and why they are definitely not friends with foxes!

The Grand
Old Duke of York

The grand old Duke of York,
He had ten thousand men.
He marched them up to the top of the hill
And he marched them down again.
When they were up, they were up.
And when they were down, they were down.
And when they were only halfway up,
They were neither up nor down.

Ring-A-Ring O' Roses

Ring-a-ring o' roses,
A pocket full of posies.
A-tishoo! A-tishoo!
We all fall down.

Pussy Cat, Pussy Cat

Pussy cat, pussy cat,
Where have you been?
I've been to London
To visit the Queen.
Pussy cat, pussy cat,
What did you there?
I frightened a little mouse
Under her chair.

Ding Dong Bell

Ding dong bell,
Pussy cat's in the well.
Who put her in?
Little Johnny Flynn.
Who pulled her out?
Little Tommy Stout.
What a naughty boy was that
To try to drown poor pussy cat,
Who never did any harm
But killed all the mice
In the farmer's barn!

The Emperor's New Clothes

Many years ago, there was a wealthy and vain emperor who only cared about fashion. Instead of spending time attending to his royal duties, he wasted hours in his private chambers, parading up and down in fancy outfits, admiring himself from every angle in all the mirrors that lined the walls.

The emperor's expensive tastes soon became famous far and wide. Merchants came to the city, hoping to sell him clothes. But even their finest wares didn't satisfy the emperor for long.

One morning, when the emperor was in a meeting with the prime minister, two strangers called at the palace.

"Your Majesty, we are master weavers," declared the taller of the two men. "Our clothes are created from the rarest fabric."

"But only the lucky few will be able to enjoy the true marvel of our creation," said the other man.

"Only the lucky few?" asked the emperor.

The two men looked at each other. "Our fabrics are so special, only the cleverest people can even see them. To anyone else, they're simply invisible. It's like there's nothing there at all!"

The prime minister started to protest at the idea, but the emperor silenced him with a wave of his hand.

"Give these fine gentlemen everything they need," said the emperor. "I want them to make me a splendid new outfit for my royal procession next week."

As the prime minister handed the two weavers twelve bags of gold, he thought that he saw them wink at each other.

A few days later, the emperor called for the prime minister.

"Go and find out how the weavers are getting on with my new suit," he cried impatiently.

The prime minister went off to see the weavers. When he entered their workshop, all he could see was an empty loom.

"What do you think?" asked the small weaver. "Look at the fabric—isn't it divine?"

The prime minister's heart sank. He couldn't see anything, but he didn't want to appear foolish.

"It's a triumph," he lied. "I shall be sure to tell the emperor what I've seen."

The day of the royal procession finally arrived. The weavers came to the emperor's chamber.

"Your Majesty," said the tall weaver, bowing. "We present your new clothes!"

The emperor made a startled squeal. He couldn't see anything. He looked at the prime minister to see what he thought. The prime minister seemed to be gazing in wonder at the new outfit.

"Thank you!" he said, too proud to admit he couldn't see any clothes. "It's perfect!"

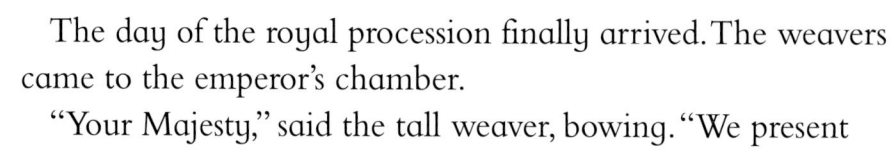

People had gathered in the streets to catch a glimpse of the emperor in his new outfit. For just one second the crowd went silent. Then, as no one wanted to look foolish, they cheered.

Just then, a small boy pushed to the front of the crowd.

"The emperor has no clothes on!" he called out. There was a pause and then the crowd burst out laughing.

The emperor gulped. The weavers had taken advantage of his own silly pride, and made him look like a fool.

Filled with shame, the emperor vowed that he would never again be so vain about his clothes!

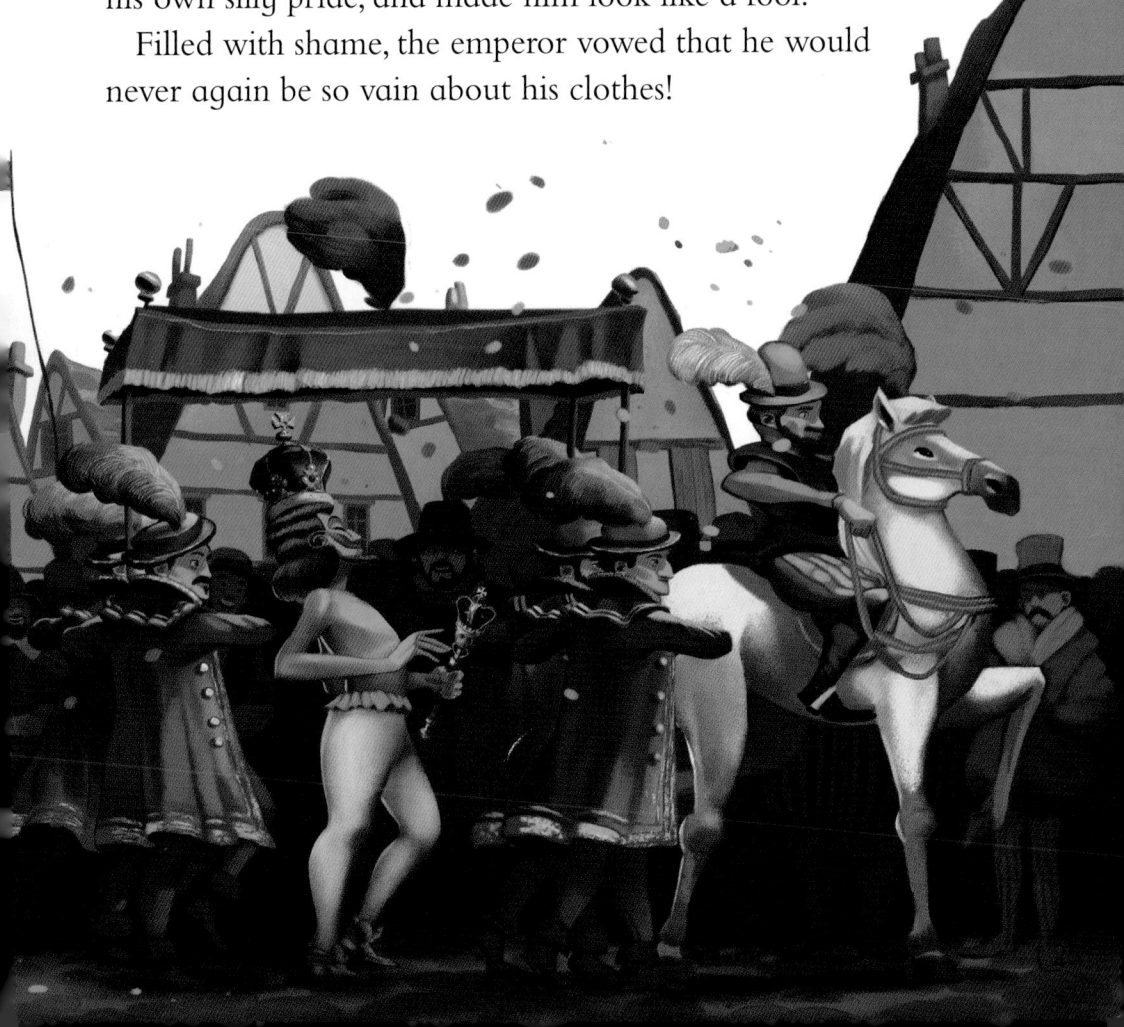

Fee, Fi, Fo, Fum!

Fee, fi, fo, fum,
I smell the blood
Of an Englishman:
Be he alive or be he dead,
I'll grind his bones
To make my bread.

Little Hare

Round about there
Sat a little hare,
The bow-wows came and chased him
Right up there!

Ten O'Clock Scholar

A diller, a dollar,
A ten o'clock scholar,
What makes you come so soon?
You used to come at ten o'clock,
But now you come at noon.

Round About

Round about the rose bush,
Three steps,
Four steps,
All the little boys and girls
Are sitting
On the doorsteps.

The Magpie

Magpie, magpie, flutter and flee,
Turn up your tail and good luck come to me.

John Smith

Is John Smith within?
Yes, that he is.
Can he set a shoe?
Aye, marry, two;
Here a nail and there a nail,
Tick, tack, too.

The Sorcerer's Apprentice

Once a young boy named Franz worked as an apprentice to a sorcerer.

Every day, the sorcerer gave Franz a long list of chores to do around the castle, while he disappeared into his workshop to chant spells, or journeyed to nearby villages.

But Franz wanted to learn magic! He knew the sorcerer kept a spell book in his workshop and he longed to read it. So he decided to sneak a look the next time the sorcerer went out.

One day, as the sorcerer was getting ready to leave the castle, he ordered Franz to clean the floor of the Great Hall.

"Fetch the water from the well with this bucket, then carry it to the big stone container in the hall," he said. "When the container is full of water, scrub the floor with this broom."

As soon as the sorcerer left, Franz rushed to get his master's spell book. Inside, Franz saw a spell that could bring objects to life.

"The broom could clean the floor by itself!" he cried, excitedly.

As Franz chanted the spell, the broom suddenly sprouted little arms and leaped into action. It carried the bucket to the well and fetched water to fill the container.

After a while, Franz noticed that the container was overflowing. There was water all over the floor.

"Stop!" he shouted. But the broom carried on.

Panicking, Franz grabbed an ax and chopped the broom into small pieces. But the little pieces of broom grew arms too. Soon there was an army of new brooms.

The sorcerer returned just as the overflowing water reached Franz's knees.

"Please forgive me, master," Franz cried. "I just wanted to try magic."

The sorcerer was angry. He chanted a spell and in an instant the brooms all vanished and the water disappeared.

"You have much to learn," the sorcerer told Franz, sternly.

"I promise to work very hard," the apprentice replied.

"Very well," replied the sorcerer, "you can start by cleaning this floor—the old-fashioned way!"

The Swallow and the Crow

One day, a young swallow landed on a branch next to a wise old crow. The swallow looked down his beak at the crow and said, "I don't think much of your stiff feathers. You should take more pride in your appearance."

The old crow was very angry and was about to fly away, when the swallow continued, "Look at me with my soft, downy feathers. They are what a well-dressed bird needs."

"Those soft feathers of yours might be all right in the spring and summer," the crow replied. "But in the winter you have to fly away to warmer countries. In the winter the trees are covered in ripe berries. I can stay here and enjoy them as I have my stiff, black feathers to keep me warm and dry."

The crow held out his wings. "What use are your fancy feathers then, Swallow?" he asked, before turning away.

And the moral of the story is: Fine-weather friends are not worth much.

The Dog and His Reflection

A hungry dog passed a butcher's store and spotted a juicy steak lying on the counter. He waited until the butcher went to the back of the store, then he ran in and stole it.

On his way home, the dog crossed a narrow bridge over a river. As he looked down into the water he saw another dog looking up at him. This dog was also carrying a piece of meat, and it looked even bigger than the one he had!

"I want that steak too," thought the greedy dog. So he jumped into the river to steal the steak from the other dog.

But as he opened his mouth to snatch the steak, the butcher's steak fell from his mouth and sank to the bottom of the river. The other dog vanished in a pool of ripples.

The greedy dog had been fooled by his own reflection, and now he was still hungry and had nothing left to eat!

And the moral of the story is: It doesn't pay to be greedy.

Sammy's Tree

Sammy the monkey sat in the biggest fruit tree in the jungle and bossed his friends around.

"No other monkeys allowed today," he would say. "Don't eat those berries. Don't sit there."

"Sammy always saves the best fruit for himself," his friends complained. "It's not fair." One by one, they stopped coming to the tree.

Eventually, no monkeys came at all.

"Where is everyone?" Sammy asked.

"They don't like being bossed around," squawked a parrot.

Sammy felt sad. He had driven his friends away. "Please tell everyone that they can eat as much as they like," he said. "I just want my friends back."

Next day, the tree was full of monkeys! Sammy didn't boss anyone around. He just laughed and played with his friends.

"Being in charge of the tree was fun," he said. "But playing with my friends is even better!"

Hide and Seek

James the meerkat played with his friend Bernard in the zoo every day. But this morning, Bernard was nowhere to be found.

"Maybe he's hiding," said James, standing on his back legs and looking all around. "I'll search the zoo."

James wriggled through the fence and scampered to the elephant house. "Have you seen Bernard?" he asked. The elephants shook their heads.

James went to see the crocodiles. "Have you seen Bernard?" he asked. They just snapped their jaws.

None of the other zoo animals had seen Bernard. James walked sadly back home and wriggled through the fence.

"SURPRISE!" shouted a friendly voice. It was Bernard, holding up a birthday cake! He'd spent the morning making the cake for his friend.

A big smile spread over James's face.

"I forgot it was my birthday," he said, blowing out the candles. "But I've already got my birthday wish. My best friend is back!"

The Stubborn Little Pig

Joe's best friend wasn't another boy or girl. It wasn't a dog or a cat. It was a pig called Samson!

"A pig can't be a real friend," said the grown-ups. But Joe didn't agree.

"He's the best pig in the world," Joe said.

They did everything together. They splashed in streams. They chased each other around meadows. And whenever Joe needed to share a secret or try out a new joke, Samson was always there to listen. There was just one problem. Samson was very, very stubborn. If he didn't want to do something, no one could make him do it.

"You can't always have your own way, you know," said Joe. "Sometimes you have to let someone else have a turn."

But Samson just gazed at him until Joe gave in and did what the little pig wanted.

One morning Joe had a bright idea.

"I know how to stop Samson from being so stubborn," he exclaimed. "He needs to go to school!"

"But how will school help?" asked Dad, while they all ate breakfast.

"Everyone has to do what the teachers say, otherwise they'll get told off," Joe explained. "School will teach Samson to do as he is told!"

So Joe put Samson on a lead and they set off together. But when they came to the road opposite the school, the little pig stopped.

"Oh no," groaned Joe. "He doesn't want to cross the road."

A policeman was passing by, and he stopped to help.

"What seems to be the problem?" he asked.

"My pig won't cross the road," said Joe. "We're going to be late for school!"

The policeman frowned at the pig. "Now then, young pig, you must cross this road. I'm a policeman, so you must do what I say."

The policeman stared at Samson, and Samson stared at the policeman. Then Samson planted his hooves firmly on the pavement and shook his little head.

"The traffic is waiting for you," said the policeman. "You have to cross the road."

It was no use. Samson didn't move one bit. The cars were hooting and a traffic jam was forming. Even worse than that, it was almost time for school to start. Joe would be in big trouble if he was late. He looked across the road and saw lots of children hurrying into the school with their friends.

Then, suddenly, Joe had an idea. He kneeled down and whispered something into Samson's ear. The little pig looked at him and gave a little snort. Then it stood up and trotted across the road. When they reached the other side, the policeman hurried after them.

"What did you say?" he asked.

Joe grinned. "I told him that he is my best friend and I need him to be at school with me," he said. "And that if he was well-behaved he could have a tasty treat!" Even stubborn little pigs like to be needed - especially if they can have a treat!

Old MacDonald Had a Farm

Old MacDonald had a farm,
Ee-i-ee-i-o!
And on that farm he had a cow,
Ee-i-ee-i-o!
With a moo-moo here,
And a moo-moo there,
Here a moo, there a moo,
Everywhere a moo-moo,
Old MacDonald had a farm,
Ee-i-ee-i-o!

Now sing it again swapping in these animals and their sounds:
Sheep (baa), horse (neigh), pig (oink), duck (quack).

Ip Dip

Ip dip, sky blue.
Who's it? Not you.
Not because you're dirty,
Not because you're clean,
My mother says you're the fairy queen.

Little Squirrel

Nibble, nibble, little squirrel,
Nibble nuts for tea.
Scamper, scamper, little squirrel,
Scamper up a tree.

Tom, Tom, the Piper's Son

Tom, Tom, the piper's son,
Stole a pig and away he ran.
The pig was eat, and Tom was beat,
And Tom went roaring down the street.

A Golden Touch

There was once a king who wished that everything he touched would turn to gold. His wish was granted by a passing fairy, and he ran around his palace turning all his belongings into gold.

"I will be so rich," he thought.

Before long, the king started to feel hungry. But when he picked up an apple, it turned to gold before it had even reached his lips.

The king began to feel very sad, but when his wife tried to comfort him with a hug, even she turned to gold.

"I never want to see gold again," sobbed the king and he wished with all his heart for things to be back to normal.

Luckily, the fairy, who had been watching all along, took pity on him. Everything changed back to the way it had been before, and the king learned a valuable lesson.

King Canute and the Ocean

King Canute was a powerful king. His courtiers were always flattering him so that they could stay in his favor.

One day, the king's courtiers persuaded him that he was so powerful that he would be able to stop the tide coming in.

King Canute, believing their flattery, went down to the beach and sat on his throne waiting for the tide to turn so that he could command it to stop.

"I command you to stop," he bellowed as the sea came in. But the tide did not stop. King Canute sat steadfast on his throne. "I command you to stop," he bellowed again, but still the sea paid no heed.

The courtiers backed away as the sea came closer, but still the king would not leave his throne. When the sea began to cover the king's feet, he realized that he was not as powerful as he'd thought. He ruled more wisely from then on.

Dotty Duck, Where Are You?

One morning, when Toby woke up, he couldn't find his favorite toys anywhere. "Perhaps they're playing hide-and-seek!" he giggled. Toby put his hands over his eyes and counted to ten.

"Coming, ready, or not!" Toby called, peeking out from between his fingers.

First Toby looked in his chest of drawers, but it was just full of pajamas. Then he rummaged in the laundry basket. "Found you, Edie!" he cried as he lifted his purple elephant from under a pile of clothes.

Next Toby peered under his bed. He could just make out a bobbly white shape in the shadows. "Good hiding, Sasha!" he said, pulling his cuddly sheep from her hiding place.

He couldn't find any more toys in his bedroom, so Toby got dressed and went downstairs. That's when he spotted Barney Bear peeping out from behind the bottom bannister.

"Just Dotty left to find now," said Toby. "Come on everyone, you can help me look." Toby gathered up his toys and began to search for Dotty, his fluffy, yellow duck.

Dotty was not in the dining room, or hiding behind the coats hanging in the hall. She was not in the closet under the stairs, or behind the cushions on the sofa.

"Perhaps she's in the garden?" thought Toby. He put on his outdoor clothes and ran outside. He looked under the slide and in his sandpit, but the only yellow thing he found was his old watering can.

"Oh, Dotty Duck! Where are you?" Toby thought.

Then Toby realized he hadn't looked in the kitchen. He opened the cupboard under the sink. There was Dotty, fast asleep, nestled among the cleaning cloths!

Toby gave her a big hug.

"You are the hide-and-seek winner," laughed Toby. "It took us so long to find you that you fell asleep!"

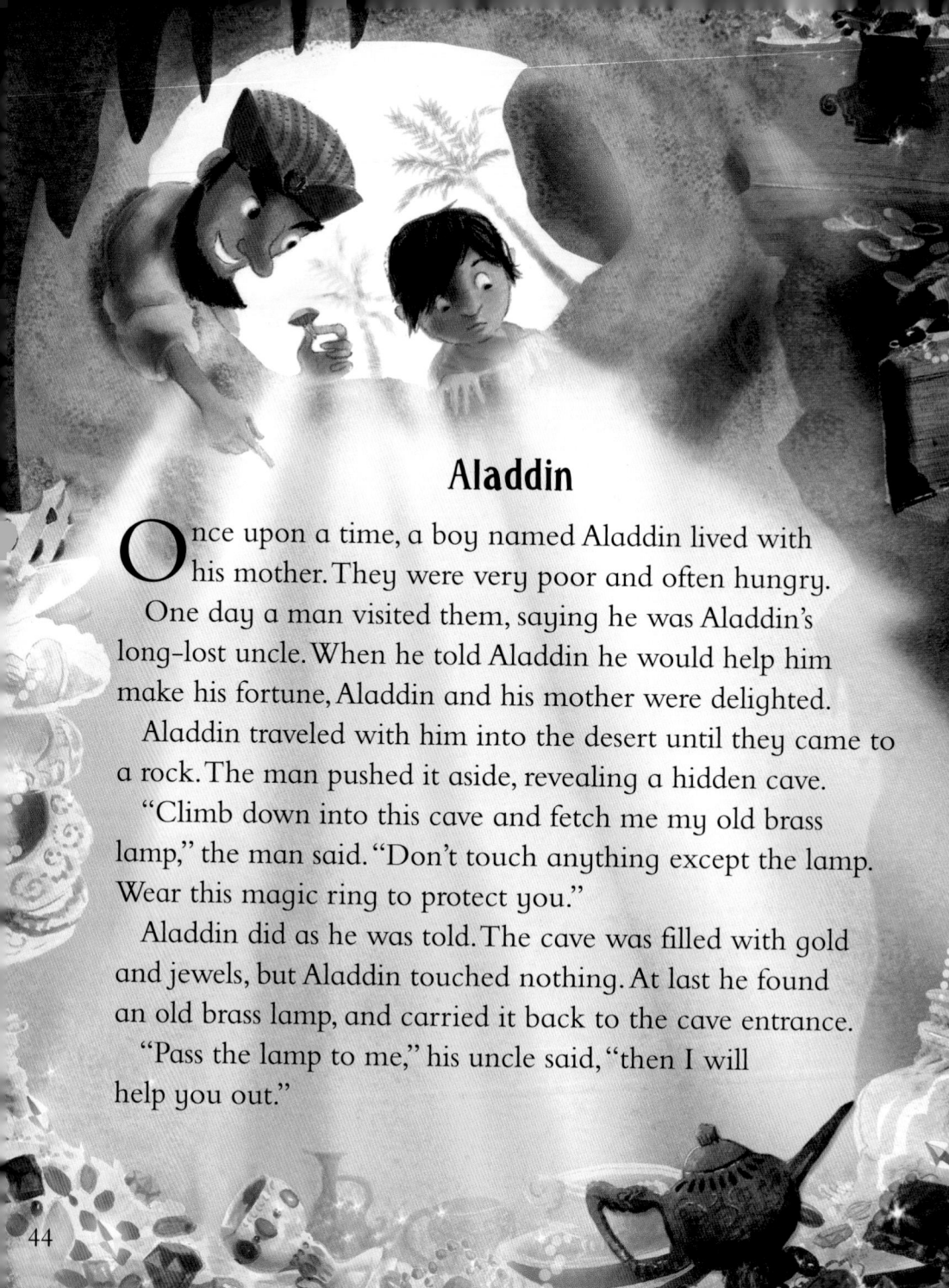

Aladdin

Once upon a time, a boy named Aladdin lived with his mother. They were very poor and often hungry.

One day a man visited them, saying he was Aladdin's long-lost uncle. When he told Aladdin he would help him make his fortune, Aladdin and his mother were delighted.

Aladdin traveled with him into the desert until they came to a rock. The man pushed it aside, revealing a hidden cave.

"Climb down into this cave and fetch me my old brass lamp," the man said. "Don't touch anything except the lamp. Wear this magic ring to protect you."

Aladdin did as he was told. The cave was filled with gold and jewels, but Aladdin touched nothing. At last he found an old brass lamp, and carried it back to the cave entrance.

"Pass the lamp to me," his uncle said, "then I will help you out."

But Aladdin wanted to be let
out first, before he gave his uncle
the lamp. This made his uncle angry.

"Fool!" the man roared, and he rolled
the rock back over the cave, trapping
Aladdin inside.

"Uncle! Let me out!" Aladdin cried.

"I'm not your uncle," said the man.
"I'm a sorcerer! Stay there for good
if you won't give me the lamp."

As Aladdin wrung his hands in
despair, he rubbed the magic ring
on his finger.

Suddenly, a genie sprang out and
asked: "What do you require, master?"

Astonished, Aladdin told the
genie to take him home. In a
flash, Aladdin was outside his
mother's house.

Still poor and hungry, Aladdin
polished the old lamp, hoping to
sell it to get money for food. But
as he rubbed the lamp clean,
another genie jumped out.

This time, Aladdin asked for
food and money so that he and
his mother could live in comfort.

Life went on happily until, one day, Aladdin fell hopelessly in love with the emperor's beautiful daughter. But how could he, Aladdin, marry a princess? Suddenly, he had an idea ... he asked the genie of the lamp for gifts to give to the princess.

When the princess thanked Aladdin for the gifts, she fell in love with him. They were soon married, and Aladdin asked the genie to build them a beautiful palace.

Hearing that a wealthy stranger had married the princess, the wicked sorcerer guessed that Aladdin must have escaped with the lamp.

One day, when Aladdin was out, the sorcerer disguised himself as a poor tradesman. He stood outside the palace calling out, "New lamps for old! New lamps for old!"

Aladdin's wife gave her husband's old brass lamp to the sorcerer, who snatched it away and rubbed the lamp. He commanded the genie to carry the palace and the princess far away.

"Oh, no!" cried Aladdin, when he discovered his wife and home gone.

Quickly, he rubbed the magic ring to make the genie appear.

"Please bring back my wife and palace!" Aladdin pleaded.

"Sorry, master, I can't!" said the genie. "I am less powerful than the genie of the lamp."

"Then take me to her and I'll win her back!" Aladdin cried.

At once, he found himself in a strange city, but outside his own palace. Through a window he saw his wife crying, and the sorcerer sleeping. Aladdin crept into the palace. He grabbed the magic lamp and rubbed it.

"What do you require, master?" asked the genie.

"Take us straight back home," Aladdin said, "and shut this wicked sorcerer in the cave for a thousand years!"

In a moment, the palace was back where it belonged. With the sorcerer gone, Aladdin and the princess were safe, and they never needed to call on the genie again.

Charley Warley

Charley Warley had a cow,
Black and white about the brow;
Open the gate and let her through,
Charley Warley's old cow.

Cushy Cow Bonny

Cushy cow bonny, let down thy milk,
And I will give thee a gown of silk;
A gown of silk and a silver key,
If thou wilt let down thy milk for me.

My Rabbit

I love my rabbit,
Who's soft and furry,
And wiggles his nose
All the time—it's his habit.

48

I Saw a Slippery, Slithery Snake

I saw a slippery, slithery snake,
Slide through the grasses, making them shake.
He looked at me with his beady eye.
"Go away from my pretty green garden," said I.
"Sssss," said the slippery, slithery snake,
As he slid through the grasses, making them shake.

Foxy's Hole

Put your finger
In Foxy's hole.
Foxy's not at home.
Foxy's out,
At the back door
A-picking at a bone.

Round About There

Round about there,
Sat a little bear,
He went to get some honey,
Right up there!

Jasper the Dancing Zebra!

Most zebras are happy galloping or grazing. But not Jasper. He loved to dance!

He tapped his hooves all through breakfast. He hip-hopped across the hills until lunchtime. He shimmied his way through the searing heat of the afternoon.

And by the light of the moon, he twirled until his legs were so tired that finally, he had to stop!

Day after day, Jasper danced. The grassy plains echoed with the sound of his clickety-clackety hooves and his happy braying as he leaped and pirouetted.

The trouble was, Jasper was so busy dancing that he forgot to do his chores.

"Jasper never helps gather the leaves and bark," moaned the other zebras.

"But he always enjoys eating them!" cried Florence.

"It's not fair! We should teach him a lesson," said Zachary.

That evening as Jasper returned home for supper, he was surprised to see the other zebras standing quietly. There were no leaves or bark on the ground.

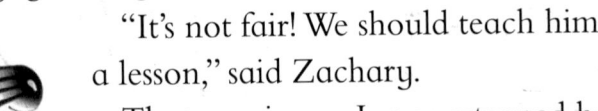

"Where's supper?" asked Jasper.

"We've already eaten," replied Florence. "You'll have to get your own."

The same thing happened the next few nights.

By the fourth evening, Jasper was feeling very unhappy. He didn't tap his hooves or sway. Tears trickled down his face.

After a while Florence came over. "We didn't mean to upset you, but we wanted to teach you a lesson," she said gently.

Jasper drooped his head. "I'm sorry. I promise I will help with the chores from now on," he whispered.

"And we really do love your dancing," said Zachary, "but just not ALL the time!"

Jasper smiled shyly at his friends. "I'll do extra jobs tomorrow," he said. "But let me do a special dance for you now, to show you how sorry I am!"

And everyone laughed, as Jasper leapt and twirled under the light of the moon.

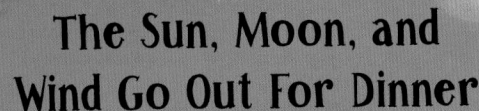

The Sun, Moon, and Wind Go Out For Dinner

A long time ago, the sun, moon, and wind went out to dinner with their friends, while their mother, a distant star, stayed at home.

Both the sun and the wind were greedy and selfish. They didn't once think about their mother, alone at home waiting for their return, while they enjoyed a great feast. The moon, on the other hand, was gentle and kind. She set aside some tasty snacks to take back to their mother.

When the sun, moon, and wind got home, their mother asked if they had brought anything back for her.

Both the sun and the wind huffed, "Of course we didn't. We went out to enjoy ourselves, not to fetch food for you!"

Tears welled up in the mother's eyes.

"Mother, don't be upset," cried the moon. "Fetch a plate and enjoy what I have brought!"

When the mother had finished her meal, she turned to the sun.

"I curse you for your selfishness," she cried. "From now on, your rays shall be hot and scorching, and shall burn all that they touch!"

And that is why the sun is so hot to this day.

"And for your greediness," she shouted at the wind, "you shall always blow, and shall parch and shrivel all living things!"

And that is why the wind always blows.

Finally, she spoke to her daughter, the moon. "You are kind and loving. You shall be ever cool and calm and bright!"

And that is why the moon's light is so soft and beautiful, even to this day.

The Bully and the Shrimp

Noah Shrimpton lived with his mom and his dad and his dog Dixie. He was a bit small for his age, but he said being small was not so bad.

When Noah and his family moved house, Noah didn't like that very much. He missed his friends and he was a bit scared about starting at a new school.

On the first day, the principal, Mrs. Johnson, took Noah to find his classroom. In the corridor, Noah bumped into a tall boy.

"What's your name?" asked the boy.

"Noah Shrimpton," said Noah with a big, friendly, I'm-new-but-nice-smile.

"SHRIMP-BOY!" jeered the boy.

Noah didn't know what to say.

"Connor!" said Mrs. Johnson. "We'll have none of that!"

Then she smiled at Noah. "Here we are. This is your teacher, Mr. Preston. I'll let him introduce you to the rest of your class."

"Good morning, everyone," said Mr. Preston. "We've got a new boy in class today—Noah Shrimpton. Let's all say hello to him."

"Hello, Noah," the class said.

"Hello, Shrimp!" called out Connor.

"Connor, stop that!" said Mr. Preston. "Noah, come and sit over here with Ellie and Will."

Noah felt his face turning red like a tomato.

Everything was better the next day. To start with, anyway. And then it happened.

Noah was having his juice when Connor bumped into him. Accidentally on purpose. Noah just knew it. Juice squirted all over his clothes.

Connor laughed and ran off grinning. Noah felt small and hot and ashamed.

"Are you okay?" asked Ellie.

"Yes," mumbled Noah. But he didn't feel okay.

After that, something bad happened every day.

Connor poured water over Noah's painting. He took Noah's bag and threw it around.

Wherever Noah went, whatever he did, there was Connor.
Being mean.

It went on ... and on ... and on ...

One break time, Ellie found Noah crying in a corner.

"Is it Connor?" she asked gently.

Noah nodded. Then he told her everything.

"Don't worry about him," Ellie said. "He's just one boy.
I'm your friend. I like you."

Noah liked Ellie too. Just talking to her made him feel better.
But Noah didn't feel better for long.

The next morning, there was Connor in front of him.
Big and mean.

"Stinky Shrimp!" yelled Connor. Noah was shaking, but he
remembered what Ellie had said. And in a voice a bit like his
own, but bigger, he shouted, "STOP! Don't call me Shrimp!
It's not my name."

Connor look surprised. He glared at Noah and ran off.

But that wasn't the end of
Connor being mean. Or of
Noah using his new, big voice.

A few days later, Connor
pushed Noah. Hard. Noah
fell backward onto the
floor. He was scared,
but he wasn't going to
let Connor get away
with it any more.

"STOP BULLYING ME!" yelled Noah, scrambling to his feet.

And Ellie was there, next to him.

"Go away, Connor," she said, "or we'll tell Mr. Preston."

All of a sudden, Connor wasn't so big and mean any more. He sort of shrank. And then he ran away.

Noah felt braver and stronger ... he'd finally stood up for himself, and it hadn't mattered that he was smaller than Connor!

Noah really hoped Connor would leave him alone now, but at the end of the school day Connor walked up to Noah. Noah's heart thumped in his chest.

"I'm sorry," Connor whispered.

"What?" said Noah.

"I'm sorry, okay?" said Connor. "I won't do it again." And then he ran off.

Noah likes his new school now. And his friends Ellie and Will.

And Connor ... well, he's not that bad either!

A, B, C

A, B, C,
Our kitty's up the tree!
And now begins,
With a sneeze and a cough
To lick her long white stockings off.
No more she'll go into the snow.
Not she, not she, not she!

Little Wind

Little wind, blow on the hill top;
Little wind, blow down the plain;
Little wind, blow up the sunshine,
Little wind, blow off the rain.

Twitching Whiskers

Twitching whiskers,
Big long ears,
Little bobtails
On their rears,
Still as statues,
One, two, three—
Then hippety hoppety,
You can't catch me!

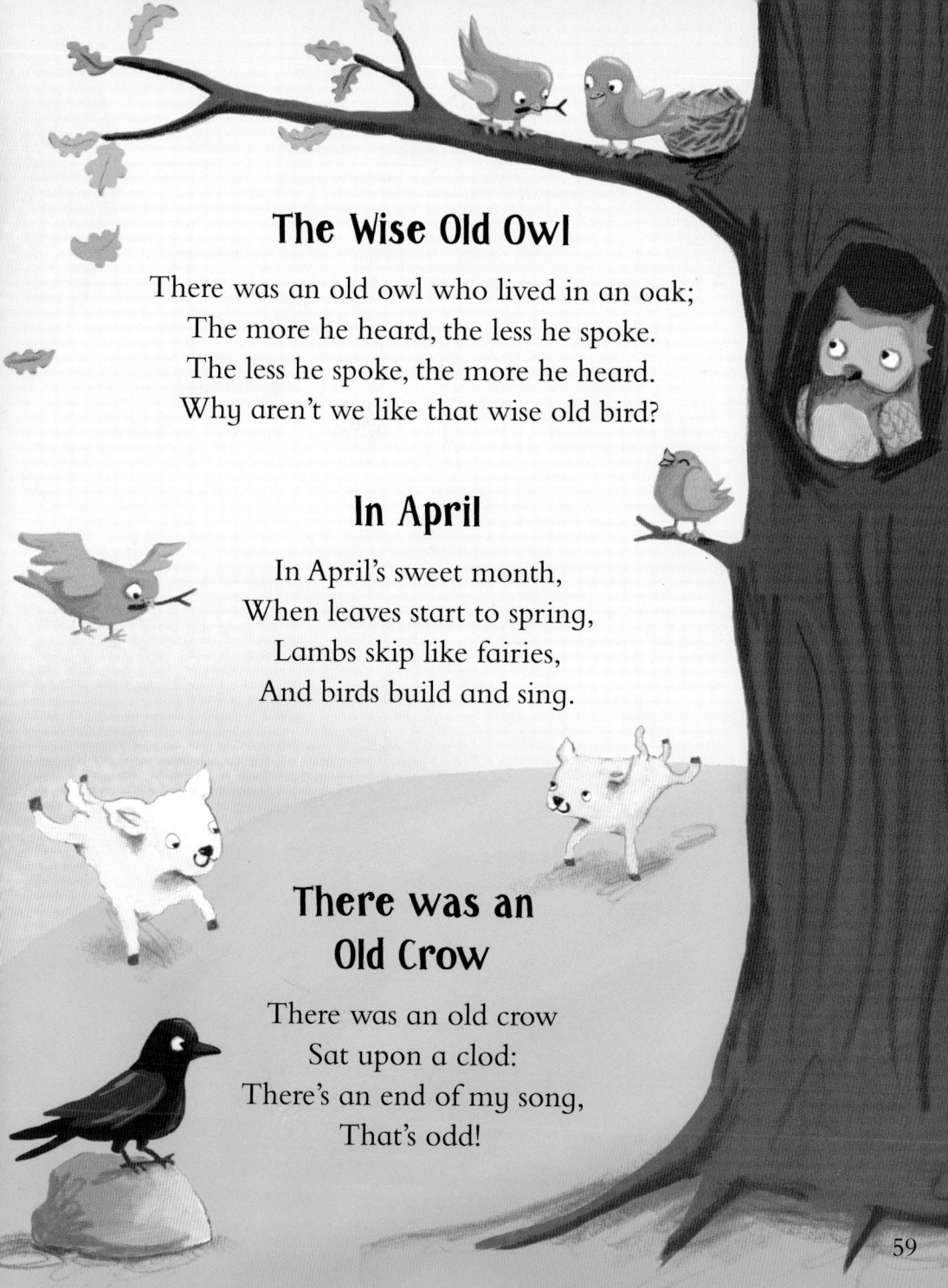

The Wise Old Owl

There was an old owl who lived in an oak;
The more he heard, the less he spoke.
The less he spoke, the more he heard.
Why aren't we like that wise old bird?

In April

In April's sweet month,
When leaves start to spring,
Lambs skip like fairies,
And birds build and sing.

There was an
Old Crow

There was an old crow
Sat upon a clod:
There's an end of my song,
That's odd!

I'll Have to Think Again

Frog was sitting on a lily pad, reading a cookbook. It was his birthday and he wanted to make a birthday cake to surprise his friends. He wrote a list of the ingredients, and set out to get them.

First, Frog went to his friend, the miller, to get a bag of flour.

"How will you get the flour home?" asked the miller.

"I'll swim up the river with it," replied Frog.

"But the flour will get wet," warned the miller, "and it will be no use to you at all."

"Oh," said Frog. "I'll have to think again."

Next, Frog went to see his friend, Brown Cow, for a bucket of her milk.

"How will you get the milk home without spilling it into the river?" asked Brown Cow.

"Oh, I don't really know," mumbled Frog. "I'll have to think again."

Frog decided to visit Speckled Hen for some eggs.

"Take as many as you need," she told Frog, "but how will you get them home?"

"I'll tuck the eggs under my chin," said Frog, happily.

"But you might drop them and then they'll break," replied Speckled Hen.

"Oh," croaked Frog, and a tear fell from the corner of his eye. "I'll just have to think again."

Frog returned to his lily pad, empty-handed and miserable. The sun was warm and he was tired, so he drifted off to sleep.

"Happy birthday to you ..."

Suddenly, Frog woke up. On the bank of the pond stood all his friends, singing. The miller was holding a birthday cake.

"But ... how?" gasped Frog.

"We wanted to surprise you," said the miller. "Brown Cow provided the milk, Speckled Hen laid some eggs, and I mixed the ingredients with my flour and baked you a cake."

"Wow! Thank you," grinned Frog. "But I was going to make a cake to surprise you."

"Well," his friends laughed, "you'll have to think again!"

I Want to be a Scary Monster!

Pog was a little purple monster with boggly eyes, two horns, and two zigzaggy wings. He was small and cute, but he wanted to be big and scary like a real monster.

Pog tried really hard to be fierce. He stomped and crashed around the house at night when the children were sleeping, shouting "ARRRGH!" and bellowing "BOO!"

But no one was ever frightened!

If the children woke up they would just mumble, "Oh, it's only Pog," and go back to sleep, and the other monsters would laugh.

At first, Pog tried not to mind that no one screamed when they saw him. But after a while, he couldn't pretend any more. He felt sad. After all, monsters weren't supposed to make people laugh!

So one night, when everything in the house was quiet, Pog crept out from his hiding place. He didn't stomp his paws. He didn't roar "BOO!" at the top of his little voice.

Slowly Pog crawled across the floor until he was crouching right behind Gloop, one of his monster friends. Silently, he stood up and flapped his wings to cast a huge frightening shadow on the wall.

"Oh, hello Pog, it's only you!" giggled Gloop. "I'd recognize those zigzaggy wings anywhere!"

"I just want to make someone scream!" Pog shouted angrily.

Gloop started to comfort his friend, when suddenly he froze on the spot. "ARRRGH! What's that?" he screamed.

Pog turned to see what had frightened his friend.

"ARRRGH!" screamed Pog. "It's a spider. SCARY!"

Pog looked at his friend. He grinned and suddenly they were both roaring with laughter.

"Oh, Pog! Look at us, scared of a little spider!" giggled Gloop. "You're really funny, you don't have to be scary. We all love you as you are."

Pog smiled shyly at his friend. Maybe real monsters didn't have to be big and scary after all.

"BOO!" he shouted at the top of his voice. "It's only me!"

I'm a Big Brother!

Luke was very excited. Grandma and Grandpa had been looking after him, but now Mommy and Daddy were home. And they had a wonderful surprise—a new baby!

"The baby is so tiny!" said Luke.

"You were this tiny once," said Daddy. "But now you're big— you're Baby's big brother!"

"Can I play with Baby?" Luke asked.

"Soon," said Mommy. "But right now Baby needs to sleep." She put the baby in a crib.

"I'll wait until the baby wakes up," Luke thought. "Then maybe we'll be able to play." But the baby woke up, and was still too tiny to play with Luke!

And the baby was still too tiny to play the next day, and the day after, and the day after that!

"You need to wait just a little bit longer," Mommy said.

All Baby seemed to do was sleep or cry or eat, or need changing.

"I wish Baby would hurry up and grow!" Luke said every day.

One morning, when Luke looked into Baby's crib, Baby was smiling—and sitting up!

Luke was so excited that he called Mommy and Daddy.

"Baby's getting bigger," they told Luke.

"Big enough to play with me?" asked Luke, holding up his toy airplane.

"Not big enough to play airplanes with you," Daddy explained. "You'll have to wait a bit longer for that.

Later, Luke watched as Daddy fed the baby. "Is Baby ever going to be big enough to play with me?" Luke asked.

"Yes," said Daddy. "You were once as little as Baby, but you got big enough to play—and Baby will too!" And Baby did start to grow. Baby grew bigger … and bigger!

Luke learned how to help dress Baby and how to help feed Baby. Baby was a very messy eater!

"Baby is very lucky to have a helpful big brother like you," said Daddy.

One afternoon, Mommy said to Luke, "Let's take Baby to the park."

"Will Baby be able to play in the sandpit with me? Or come on the swings?" Luke asked.

"Not just yet," said Mommy. "But Baby would love to watch you! A big brother can show Baby all sorts of things."

At the park, Luke rushed to the sandpit. "I'll show Baby how to make a sand castle!" he said.

Baby happily watched Luke build a wonderful sand castle.

"It's even more fun when Baby watches," Luke said.

"I think Baby is having fun too!" said Mommy.

That night, Luke said he would like to help Mommy give Baby a bath.

While Mommy washed Baby, Luke sailed a boat through the bubbles and made little splashes in the water.

Baby laughed and kicked and splashed too. It was lots of fun—almost like playing with Baby!

A few days later, Luke was playing with his train in the living room. Suddenly, Baby crawled over and grabbed the engine!

"Mommy! Daddy!" cried Luke. "Baby is taking my train! Make Baby stop!"

"I think Baby is trying to tell you something," Mommy said.

"What?" Luke asked.

"I think," said Mommy, "that Baby is saying ... 'I'm ready to play with you now!'"

"Hooray!" cried Luke. He ran to the toybox and picked up a soft, squishy ball.

"Catch!" said Luke, as he rolled the ball to Baby. Baby laughed and tried to catch the ball. Luke rolled the ball to Baby again, and this time Baby grabbed it.

Baby laughed, and Luke laughed too.

He rolled the ball to Baby again and again. "I think," Luke said to Mommy and Daddy, "that being a big brother is going to be lots of fun from now on!"

And it was!

Billy's First Day at School

Billy loved to do new things, but he couldn't think of anything new to do today. "I've tried swinging upside down," he said to Mom. "I've made mud pies, learned magic tricks and walked on stilts. What next?"

"Have you forgotten?" asked Mom. "You're starting school today."

"What if there's nothing new to do there?" Billy worried.

"You might be surprised," his mom said.

Billy's teacher was called Mr. Lemon. "Today you'll learn to write your own name on all your books," he said. "Then you'll try rope climbing, then I'll teach you to play a song on the piano."

It was an amazing day. Billy learned five new games, made six friends, and even made a magic potion that bubbled all over the classroom!

"How was your first day?" Mom asked at home time.

"AWESOME!" Billy replied, grinning. "I'll never run out of new things to do at school!"

Poor George!

Absolutely nothing about George's life was normal. You see, George's mom was a witch and his dad was a wizard. George's clothes weren't washed in a machine—they were washed by magic! But whenever George tried the washing spell, it went a bit wrong. That's how his sports clothes turned bright pink. Poor George!

George's dinner wasn't cooked in the oven—it was cooked by magic. But when George cooked dinner, the spells got mixed up. That's why he had blue burgers and red yogurt for tea. Poor George!

One evening, George had a brainwave. He could do his homework by magic!

"Abracadabra!" BANG! One of his school books turned into a purple frog. George tried again. PUFF! Another book became a green parrot. George sighed, dropped the wand, and picked up a pen.

"Maybe I'll do my homework the normal way," he said. Poor George!

Seven Ravens

Once there lived a man and a woman who had seven sons, but longed for a daughter. When their eighth child was a girl, they were very happy. At last their wish had come true.

The beautiful baby girl was a thirsty little thing, so the seven sons were sent out to the well to fetch water.

"Take this silver cup and fill it for the baby," said their mother. But the silver cup fell into the well with a splash! The boys were too frightened to go home.

When they didn't return, their father cursed them. "May those lazy good-for-nothing boys become ravens!" he shouted. As soon as the words left his mouth, he saw seven ravens flying off into the distance. Although he regretted his words, it was too late to undo his curse.

When the little girl grew older, her sad mother told her all about her seven lost brothers. The brave girl vowed to find them and bring them home.

She set off, taking her mother's ring as a keepsake, and searched the world over.

"Where are my seven brothers?" she called up to the heavens. The stars could see that the poor girl was in despair and took pity on her. They sent down a magical key and, as the girl picked it up, she heard these words:

"Follow our light to a mountain of glass,
You'll find your raven brothers at last."

After walking for many days, the young girl finally reached the glass mountain. Using the key, she entered a crystal cave and, although nobody was there, she noticed seven little plates and cups laid out with food and drink.

Being very hungry, she took a bite from each plate and a sip from each cup. Her ring fell into the last cup but, before she could pick it up again, she heard the swish of wings. She hid behind a door and watched seven ravens swoop down.

Each raven noticed that some of their food and drink was missing. Then the last raven found the ring in his cup and recognized it as his mother's.

"If only our little sister has come to find us," he exclaimed, "for then we could return home with her."

On hearing this, their brave little sister cried out with joy. As soon as they saw her, the ravens turned back into men.

Reunited at long last, they returned home and lived happily ever after.

The Fuzzy Caterpillar

The fuzzy caterpillar
Curled up on a leaf,
Spun her little chrysalis
And then fell fast asleep.
While she was a-sleeping
She dreamed that she could fly,
And later when she woke up
She was a butterfly!

Cobweb Races

No wonder spiders wear bare feet
To run their cobweb races.
Suppose they had to have eight shoes,
How would they tie their laces?

The Snail

The snail he lives in his hard round house,
In the orchard, under the tree:
Says he, "I have but a single room;
But it's large enough for me."

Flying High, Swooping Low

Flying high, swooping low,
Loop-the-loop and round they go.
Catching currents, soaring fast,
Feathered friends come sweeping past.

The Pigeon

A pigeon and a pigeon's son
Once went to town to buy a bun.
They couldn't decide on a plum or plain,
And so they flew back home again.

What Does the Donkey Say?

What does the donkey say?
Hee-haw, hee-haw.
What does the blackbird say?
Caw, caw, caw.
What does the cat say?
Meow, meow, meow.
What does the dog say?
Bow-wow, bow-wow.

The Lion and the Mouse

Once upon a time, there was a huge lion who lived in a dark den in the middle of the jungle. If Lion didn't get enough sleep, he became extremely grumpy.

One day, while Lion lay sleeping as usual, a little mouse thought he'd take a shortcut home straight through the lion's den.

"He's snoring so loudly," thought Mouse. "He'll never hear me."

But as he hurried past, he accidentally ran over Lion's paw.

"How dare you wake me up!" Lion roared angrily, grabbing the mouse. "I will eat you for my supper."

"Please," cried Mouse. "I didn't mean to wake you up. I'm too small to make a good meal for someone as mighty as you. Let me go and I promise to help you one day."

Lion laughed loudly. "You're too small to help someone as big as me," he said scornfully, but he opened his paw. "Go home, little mouse."

Mouse looked at Lion in surprise.

"You have made me laugh, so I will let you go," Lion explained. "But hurry, before I change my mind."

"Thank you!" squeaked Mouse gratefully, and he ran home.

A few days later, Lion was hunting in the jungle when he got tangled in a hunter's snare net. He was so angry that he let out the loudest of roars.

"Lion must be in trouble!" squeaked Mouse.

When he found the lion, Mouse started gnawing through the net. Before long, there was a big hole in the net, and Lion climbed through.

"Thank you," he said humbly. "I was wrong to laugh at you. You saved my life today."

Mouse smiled. "You were kind enough to let me go before," he squeaked. "It was my turn to help you."

And from that day on the huge, mighty lion and the tiny, mighty mouse became the best of friends.

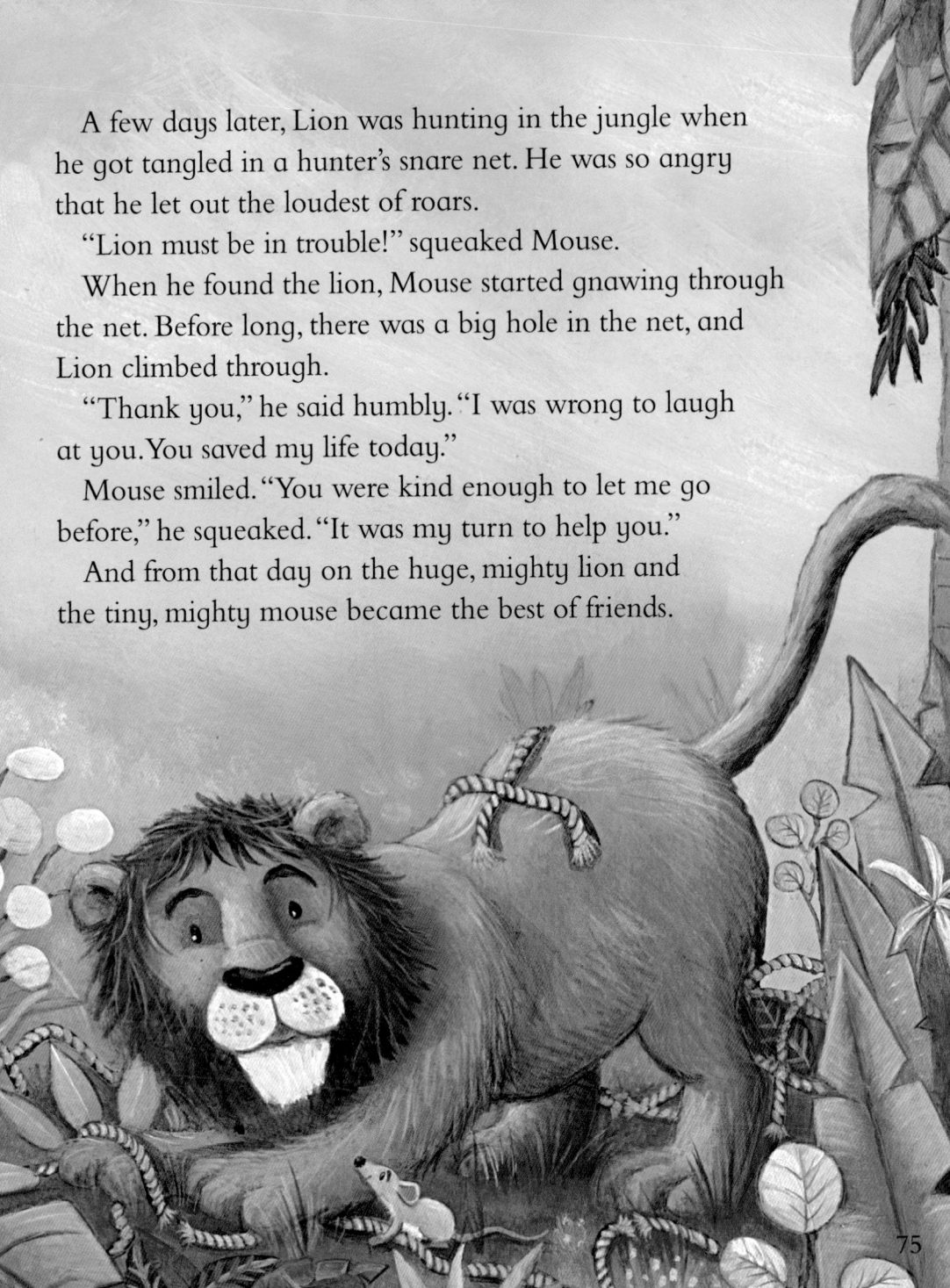

The Ugly Duckling

Once there was a proud and happy duck. "I have seven beautiful eggs and soon I will have seven beautiful ducklings," she told her friends on the riverbank.

A while later she heard a CRACK! One beautiful duckling popped her little head out of a shell. And then another ... and another ... until she had six beautiful little ducklings, drying their fluffy yellow wings in the spring air.

"Just one egg left," quacked Mother Duck, "and it's a big one!"

For a while, nothing happened. Then, at last, the big egg began to hatch.

Tap, tap, tap! Out came a beak.

Crack, crack, crack! Out popped a head.

Crunch, crunch, crunch! Out came the last duckling.

"Oh, my!" gasped Mother Duck, "Isn't he ... different?"

The last little duckling did look strange. He was bigger than the other ducklings and he didn't have such lovely yellow feathers.

"That's okay," said Mother Duck. "You may look different, but you're special to me."

When Mother Duck took her little ducklings for a swim, each one landed in the river with a little plop. But the ugly duckling fell over his big feet and landed in the water with a big SPLASH! The other ducklings laughed at their clumsy brother.

"Hush now, little ones," said Mother Duck. "Stick together and stay behind me!"

Back at the nest, the ducklings practiced their quacking.

"Quack, quack, quackety-quack!" said the ducklings, repeating after Mother Duck.

"Honk! Honk!" called the ugly duckling.

The other ducklings all quacked with laughter.

The ugly duckling hung his head in shame.

"I'll never fit in," he thought sadly.

The next day, Mother Duck took her little ones out for another swim. The little ducklings stayed close to her while the ugly duckling swam alone.

"What kind of a bird are you?" asked some geese, who had landed on the river nearby.

"I'm a duckling," he replied. "My family have left me all alone."

The geese felt sorry for the ugly duckling, and asked him to go with them. But the ugly duckling was too afraid to leave his river, so he stayed put.

When Mother Duck wasn't looking, the other ducklings teased their ugly brother.

"Look at his dull, gray feathers," said one of his sisters unkindly, admiring her own reflection in the water. "Mine are so much prettier."

The ugly duckling swam away and looked at his reflection.

"I don't look the same as them," he thought, sadly.

So he swam down the river and didn't stop until he'd reached a place he had never seen before. "I'll stay here," he decided.

Summer turned to autumn. The sky became cloudy and the river murky. But still the ugly duckling swam alone in his quiet part of the river.

Snow fell heavily that winter and the ugly duckling was cold and lonely. The river was frozen solid.

"At least I can't see my ugly reflection any more," he thought.

Spring arrived at last and the ice thawed.

Some magnificent white ducks arrived on the river, and swam toward the ugly duckling.

"You're very big ducks," he said, nervously.

"We're not ducks," laughed the elegant creatures. "We're swans—just like you!"

Puzzled, the ugly duckling looked at his reflection in the river and was surprised to see beautiful white feathers and an elegant long neck.

"Is that really me?" he asked.

"Of course," they told him. "You are a truly handsome swan!"

The handsome young swan joined his new friends and glided gracefully back up the river with them.

When he swam past a family of ducks, Mother Duck recognized her ugly duckling straight away. "I always knew he was special," she said.

And the beautiful young swan drifted by, proudly ruffling his spectacular white feathers and holding his elegant head high.

79

The King's White Elephant

Once upon a time, there lived a kind-hearted, magnificent white elephant. He dearly loved his old, blind mother and took great care of her. They lived in a cave beside a beautiful lake surrounded by lovely pink lotus flowers.

One day, a forester lost his way in the forest and was terrified to find himself alone in the thick woods. He began to weep and call for help. The elephant was in the forest gathering fruit for his mother, when he heard the man's cries of distress. He showed him the way out of the forest. The forester thanked the elephant and happily went home.

After some days, the forester heard the news that King Brahmadutta's personal elephant had died. He was looking for a new elephant. The forester remembered the kind white elephant, and thought that if he told the king about him, he would certainly get a reward.

The next day, the forester led the king to the white elephant's cave. The white elephant was upset at the forester's selfishness, but he didn't put up a fight because he didn't want to hurt anyone. He was led away to the king's palace. The elephant's poor mother was devastated that the king had taken away her son. She lay down in the cave and cried bitterly.

Meanwhile, the white elephant was given a grand welcome in the royal elephant compound. The keepers laid out a feast for him, but he didn't touch the food. He just stood there with a sad expression on his face.

The king came to see what was wrong. The elephant told the king about his blind mother and how she couldn't survive on her own and would die.

The kind-hearted king was touched by the elephant's story, and allowed him to return to his mother.

The white elephant took good care of his mother until the day she died. The king often used to visit him in the forest. And when the white elephant died himself, the king erected a statue of him by the side of the lake and held an annual elephant festival there in his memory.

There Was a King

There was a king, and he had three daughters,
And they all lived in a basin of water;
The basin's bended,
My story's ended.
If the basin had been stronger,
My story would be longer.

King Boggen

King Boggen, he built a fine new hall;
Pastry and piecrust, that was the wall;
The windows were made of black pudding and white,
Roofed with pancakes—you never saw the like.

I Had A Little Nut Tree

I had a little nut tree,
Nothing would it bear,
But a silver nutmeg
And a golden pear.

The King of Spain's daughter
Came to visit me,
All for the sake
Of my little nut tree!

King Stephen

King Stephen was a worthy king
As ancient bards do sing;
He brought three pecks of barley-meal,
To make a bag-pudding.

Robin Hood, Robin Hood

Robin Hood, Robin Hood,
Is in the mickle wood!
Little John, Little John,
He to the town is gone.

Robin Hood

Robin Hood has gone to the wood;
He'll come back again if we are good.

Fire Flyer!

Ben was the oldest engine in the fire station. He should have been happy, because he loved his job. But lately, all the newer engines had been getting to the fires first.

"I haven't put out a fire for ages," Ben told his friend Harry Helicopter. "The newer engines are so much faster than me and by the time I arrive, they have already put out the fire."

Harry thought hard. Then he flashed his lights. "I've got an idea," he exclaimed. "Flying is much quicker than driving. If you could fly to the fires, you'd always get there first."

"But how can a fire engine fly?" Ben asked. "It's impossible. Engines don't have wings."

"I'll carry you," said Harry. "I'm strong, and I'll get you to the fire quickly."

Suddenly, the fire alarm started to ring. Ben felt worried. He had never flown before, but he really wanted to put out the fire, so he let Harry lift him up. Soon they were whizzing across town, high above the narrow streets and traffic jams.

"There's the fire!" Ben cried.

A huge factory was engulfed in flames. SPLOOSH! SQUIRT! Ben used his hose to put out the fire, and then Harry lowered him to the ground.

The newer fire engines raced up to the factory. "Thank goodness you got here so fast!" they gasped. "That fire was spreading quickly."

The fire officers gave Ben and Harry three cheers. "From now on, we'll always keep Harry nearby to make sure that Ben can reach the fires," they said. "Three cheers for brave Ben and Harry!"

Troll ... Two ... Three ... Four ...

Trolls like to laze about twiddling their toes,
Picking their noses and having a doze.
They love to creep up behind goats and go, "Boo!"
Except for one sad, lonely troll: Boogaloo.

The other trolls tried but could not understand
Why Boogaloo felt so alone in Troll Land.
"All I want is a friend," he thought with a sigh,
And just then, a shiny red THING floated by!

He ran after the thing and was running so fast,
He went straight by the sign that
NO troll should go past!

A second troll followed behind Boogaloo,
Thinking, "Where is he going? I want to go too!"
They walked through the keep-out clouds straight to a place
Where a human being stood with a very shocked face.

The human being screamed, "I SEE TROLLS!" very loud,
And fled as a third troll came out of the cloud.
Another troll—number four—followed them too,
Marching in line right behind Boogaloo.

And before you could say "boogie-boo!" there were crowds
Of curious trolls popping out through the clouds.
Trolls foul and furry were marching along,
Singing their favorite troll marching song ...

"Troll, two, three, four ... we're the trolls who grunt and snore.
Troll, two, three, four ... we don't know, there might be more,
But we can only count to four!"

The humans were frightened—the trolls looked so scary,
So scruffy and smelly, so horrid and hairy!
As the trolls passed a park, Boogaloo sneaked away.
He opened the gate and ran in to play!

In a house just nearby, a boy stood on a chair.
He whispered, "Hey, look, there's a troll over there!
He looks a bit lonely, I'll just go and see
If maybe he'd play with somebody like me."

"Hello," said the boy, "my name's Jake. Who are you?"
The little troll smiled and said, "Boogaloo!"
"Come play on this whizz-thing!" Boogaloo cried.
"All right," answered Jake. "But we call it a slide."

"Will you be my very best friend, Boogaloo?"
"Yes please!" the troll answered. "Will you be mine too?"
And humans and trolls all crept closer to see
What very best friends trolls and humans could be.

There is nothing between trolls and humans today:
The signs all came down, the clouds drifted away.
Together they play with balloons and toy boats
And no one is frightened ... not even the goats!

The Pied Piper of Hamelin

A long time ago, the little town of Hamelin was overrun by rats.

One day, a stranger came to see the mayor. "I will rid your town of rats if you pay me one hundred gold coins," he said.

The mayor agreed and so the stranger began to play an enchanting tune on a pipe. The rats followed the piper, who led them into a river where they drowned. But when the piper went to ask for his money, the mayor refused to pay.

The next day, the piper returned and played his tune again. This time it was not rats that followed him, but children. "When you pay me what you owe, I will return the children," he told the mayor.

The people of Hamelin were furious. "Pay the piper what he is owed," they shouted.

The mayor paid the piper, and the children were returned to their parents.

The people of Hamelin chose a new mayor and, from then on, Hamelin thrived.

The Sun and the Wind

One day, not so long ago, the sun and the wind were having an argument.

"I am stronger than you," said the sun.

"Nonsense," said the wind. "I am far stronger than you."

"See that man down there?" the sun asked the wind, "I am so strong that I bet I could get that coat off him."

"You're not strong enough to do that," said the wind. "I could easily get that coat off him."

"All right," said the sun. "You go first."

So the wind blew with all his might and strength. Leaves blew off the trees and tiles blew off the rooftops. But the man only pulled his coat more tightly around him. The wind could not get the coat off the man.

"Now it's my turn," said the sun. And he shone down on the man. The strength of the sun was so fierce that the man quickly became very hot. He became so hot that he took off his coat and slung it over his shoulder.

"I win!" said the sun, shining brightly, and the wind sighed huffily in defeat.

Green Cheese

Green cheese,
Yellow laces,
Up and down
The market places.

Pit, Pat

Pit, pat, well-a-day,
Little Robin flew away;
Where can little robin be?
Gone into the cherry tree.

The Wind

Who has seen the wind? Neither I nor you;
But when the leaves hang trembling
The wind is passing through.

Who has seen the wind? Neither you nor I;
But when the trees bow down their heads
The wind is passing by.

Bagpipes

Puss came dancing out of a barn
With a pair of bagpipes under her arm;
She could sing nothing but, "Fiddle cum fee,
The mouse has married the humble-bee."
Pipe, cat! Dance, mouse!
We'll have a wedding at our good house.

Mother?

"Mother, may I go out to swim?"
"Yes, my darling daughter.
Fold your clothes up neat and trim,
But don't go near the water."

Shrovetide

Once, twice, thrice,
I give thee warning,
Please to make pancakes
Again in the morning.

93

The Town and the Country Mouse

Once there were two little mice. One lived in the town, and the other in the country.

One day, Town Mouse visited Country Mouse's home. It was small and dark—not at all like Town Mouse's home.

After lunch, the two friends went for a walk. First, they strolled into a field.

"Moo!"

"What was that?" asked Town Mouse nervously.

"Just a cow," replied his friend.

So they carried on walking toward a peaceful pond.

"Hiss!"

"What was that?" asked Town Mouse, quivering from nose to tail.

"Just a goose," replied his friend.

So the two mice strolled on into a shady wood.

"Twit-twoo!"

"What was that?" yelped Town Mouse.

"An owl!" cried Country Mouse. "Quick! Run before it eats you!"

So they ran until they found a hedge to hide in.

"I don't like the country!" Town Mouse cried. "Come with me to the town. It's much better!" So they went.

Town Mouse's home was huge and grand—not at all like Country Mouse's home.

After dinner, the friends went for a walk, passing some shops on the way.

"Beep-beep!"

"What's that?" asked Country Mouse fearfully.

"Just a car," said his friend.

The mice carried on, strolling down a wide road.

"Wee-you! Wee-you!"

"What's that?" asked Country Mouse, his whiskers twitching.

"Just a fire engine," his friend replied.

As they pitter-pattered home, they passed a pretty garden.

"Meow!"

"What's that?" squeaked Country Mouse.

"A cat!" cried Town Mouse. "Quick! Run before it eats you!"

So they ran all the way back to Town Mouse's house.

"I don't like the town! I'm going home," cried Country Mouse.

"But what about that owl?" asked Town Mouse.

"It doesn't scare me!" cried Country Mouse. "What about that cat?"

"It doesn't scare me!" cried Town Mouse.

The two mice knew they would never agree. So they shook hands and went their separate ways.

And they lived happily ever after, each in his own way.

Goldy's Fishy Adventure

Goldy the fish lived deep, deep under the sea. His home was so far down that there was hardly any light at all. Everything around Goldy was gloomy and dark. In fact, the only thing that wasn't dull was Goldy! He was as bright as the sun, and his smile was even brighter. But Goldy had never seen the sun. He had never seen the sky or felt the wind on his face.

"What is it like up there?" Goldy asked his friend the crab.

The crab tapped his claws on a rock.

"It's very hot and bright," he said. "And it's dangerous, because there are humans up there. They are all cruel. They want to catch fish and crabs and eat them up."

The other deep-sea creatures gathered around too.

"He's right," said the jellyfish. "Humans are not our friends."

"I was caught in a net once," said a swordfish with a shiver. "I had to cut my way out."

"It sounds amazing up there," said Goldy. "I want to see the beautiful sun and watch the waves. I even want to see some humans. They can't all be bad."

The other creatures shook their heads and stared at Goldy.

"Going to the surface is too risky," said the crab.

But Goldy thought about the sunshine and the waves and the breeze, and he couldn't stay down in the deep waters any longer. He swam up, up, UP!

The water began to get lighter. Everything started to look a little less gloomy. Then it looked a LOT less gloomy. And then, at last, Goldy's head broke through the water and he felt the cool wind on his scales. A huge smile spread across his face. His colorful scales sparkled in the sunshine, and his smile was dazzling. It was even spotted by a family fishing from a boat.

"What a beautiful fish!" said the little boy. "He's awesome!"

"Let's catch him," said the boy's sister, and their father agreed. The girl cast her line into the water. It bobbed toward Goldy.

Goldy gazed at the fishing line. He had never seen one before, and he didn't know what it was. He swam a little closer. He could see the boy watching him.

"Swim away!" he shouted to Goldy. "Stay free!"

Goldy plunged down into the water, away from the fishing line. The girl and her father groaned, but the boy smiled. When Goldy was at a safe distance, he turned and smiled too. He knew that he had made a human friend. Then he turned and dived down, down, down to his gloomy home.

Everything seemed different now that he had seen the surface. His friends were waiting for him. When they saw him come back safely, they cheered and danced around.

"How did you stay safe?" asked the crab.

"It was all thanks to a human boy," said Goldy. "Not all humans want to catch fish. Some people just want to be friends!"

Three Young Rats

Three young rats with black felt hats,
Three young ducks with white straw flats,
Three young dogs with curling tails,
Three young cats with demi-veils,
Went out to walk with two young pigs
In satin vests and sorrel wigs;
But suddenly it chanced to rain,
And so they all went home again.

Humpty Dumpty

Humpty Dumpty sat on a wall,
Humpty Dumpty had a great fall;
All the king's horses and all the king's men
Couldn't put Humpty together again.

We're All in the Dumps

We're all in the dumps,
For diamonds and trumps,
The kittens are gone to St. Paul's,
The babies are bit,
The moon's in a fit,
And the houses are built without walls.

Tweedle-dum and Tweedle-dee

Tweedle-dum and Tweedle-dee
Agreed to have a battle,
For Tweedle-dum said Tweedle-dee
Had spoiled his nice new rattle.
Just then flew down a monstrous crow,
As big as a tar-barrel,
Which frightened both the heroes so,
They quite forgot their quarrel.

Daffy-Down-Dilly

Daffy-Down-Dilly
Has come up to town
In a yellow petticoat
And a green gown.

Little Tommy Tittlemouse

Little Tommy Tittlemouse
Lived in a little house;
He caught fishes
In other men's ditches.

Captain Rustybeard's New Rules

Captain Rustybeard loved being a pirate ... mostly. "I just wish there weren't so many rules," he grumbled, thumping the Pirate Rulebook. He didn't seem to be allowed to do any of the things he really wanted.

"I'd like a pet dog," Captain Rustybeard said one day.

"Pirates don't have dogs," said the first mate, looking astonished. "A parrot is the only pet for a pirate captain. Look in the rulebook."

"My feet ache," said Captain Rustybeard another day. "I think I'll get myself a nice, comfy pair of slippers."

"Pirates don't wear slippers!" said the boatswain in a shocked voice. "They wear stiff leather boots. It's rule number five."

"But leather boots give me blisters," Captain Rustybeard grumbled.

One sunny afternoon, Captain Rustybeard looked down through the clear water and saw dozens of oyster shells on the seabed.

"Let's dive for pearls!" he cried.

"Pirates don't dive for pearls," said the cabin boy with a gasp. "We're supposed to rob them from other ships. Do you know the Pirate Rulebook at all?"

Captain Rustybeard flung the rulebook down on the deck and jumped up and down on it.

"I'm tired of being told what pirates don't do!" he roared. "From now on, I'm going to decide on the rules!"

At first, the crew were worried. What if other pirates laughed at them? But after a while, they started to enjoy themselves. After all, sheepskin slippers were a lot cozier than leather boots. The Captain's pet dog knew some good tricks, and they found more pearls by diving for them than by robbing ships.

"This is the life for me!" exclaimed Captain Rustybeard, wiggling his toes in his new slippers.

Soon, every pirate on the high seas had heard about Captain Rustybeard's new rules, and can you guess what?

They all wanted to join his crew!

103

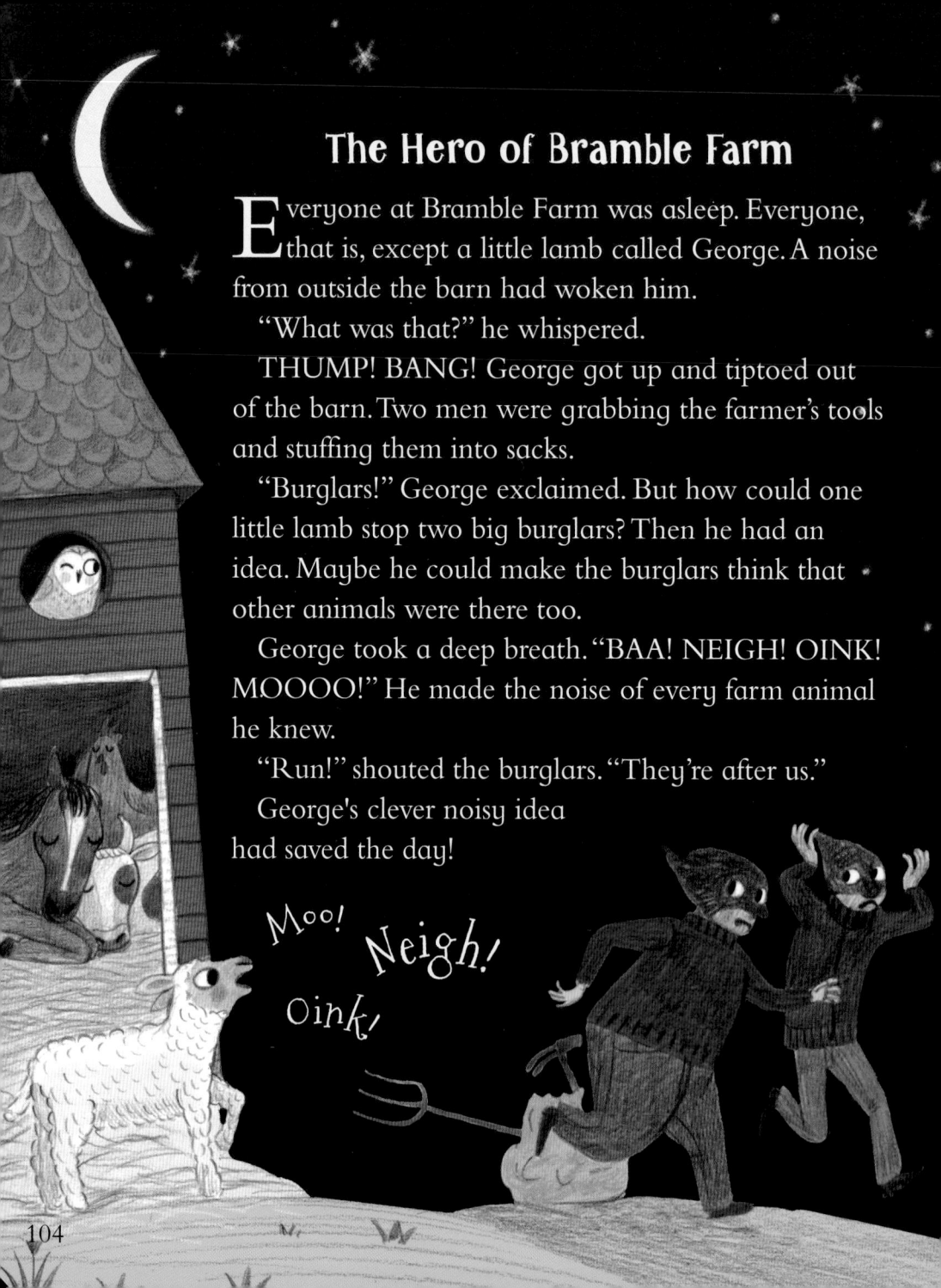

The Hero of Bramble Farm

Everyone at Bramble Farm was asleep. Everyone, that is, except a little lamb called George. A noise from outside the barn had woken him.

"What was that?" he whispered.

THUMP! BANG! George got up and tiptoed out of the barn. Two men were grabbing the farmer's tools and stuffing them into sacks.

"Burglars!" George exclaimed. But how could one little lamb stop two big burglars? Then he had an idea. Maybe he could make the burglars think that other animals were there too.

George took a deep breath. "BAA! NEIGH! OINK! MOOOO!" He made the noise of every farm animal he knew.

"Run!" shouted the burglars. "They're after us."

George's clever noisy idea had saved the day!

Moo! Neigh! Oink!

Team Tractor

There were lots of big, shiny tractors in the store. Farmers came in every day to buy them. But one tractor never seemed to get noticed.

"I wish I could work on a farm," said the little green tractor. "My cab is shiny and new. But no one looks at me."

One day, a farmer came in with his son Jamie. The farmer's tractor had broken, and he needed a new one to plant a field with seeds.

"Please!" thought the little green tractor. "Please buy me!"

The farmer was looking at the big machines, but Jamie stared at the little tractor. "You're just the right size for our little farm," he grinned, and called his dad over to see it.

"What a perfect tractor," the farmer agreed.

So they took the little green tractor home, and together they planted the field of seeds in record time!

There Was an Old Woman
Who Lived in a Shoe

There was an old woman who lived in a shoe,
She had so many children she didn't know what to do;
She gave them some broth without any bread;
And scolded them soundly and put them to bed.

There Was an Old Woman
and Nothing She Had

There was an old woman
And nothing she had,
And so this old woman
Was said to be sad.
She'd nothing to ask,
And nothing to give,
And when she did die
She'd nothing to leave.

There Was an Old Woman
and What Do You Think?

There was an old woman, and what do you think?
She lived upon nothing but victuals and drink:
Victuals and drink were the chief of her diet;
This tiresome old woman could never be quiet.

There Was an Old Woman
Went Up in a Basket

There was an old woman went up in a basket,
Seventy times as high as the moon;
What she did there I could not but ask it,
For in her hand she carried a broom.
"Old woman, old woman, old woman," said I,
"Whither, oh whither, oh whither so high?"
"To sweep the cobwebs from the sky,
And I shall be back again, by and by."

There Was an Old Woman
Lived Under the Hill

There was an old woman
Lived under the hill,
And if she's not gone
She lives there still.

There Was an Old Woman
Called Nothing-at-all

There was an old woman called Nothing-at-all,
Who rejoiced in a dwelling exceedingly small;
A man stretched his mouth to its utmost extent,
And down at one gulp house and old woman went.

Noah's Ark

Long, long ago, when the world was still new, God looked down and saw that the people on Earth had become wicked. They had forgotten that God wanted them to be good. Instead of helping each other, they spent all their time fighting and hurting one another.

All this wickedness made God unhappy.

But an old man named Noah remembered God. Noah and his family spent their days working hard and being kind to their neighbors and to each other. God was pleased with Noah and his family.

One day, God spoke to Noah.

"The world is too full of wickedness," God said, "and I am going to send a flood to destroy the Earth and everyone on it. But I will keep you and your family safe."

"What must I do?" asked Noah.

"Build a big boat called an ark," said God. "It must be big enough to hold you and your whole family, and two of every animal in the world."

Noah got to work right away. His sons, Ham, Shem, and Japheth, all helped.

They planned and measured ... they chopped and sawed ... they hammered and heaved ... and together, they built a great, strong ark.

At last the ark was ready. Noah's wife, his sons, and his sons' wives all climbed aboard.

Then Noah gathered two of every animal on Earth—every creature that hopped or walked or crawled or flew came to board the ark.

There were cats and bats and rats, monkeys and donkeys, hooting owls and wolves that howled, kangaroos and kinkajous, big baboons and little raccoons—so many animals, of all sorts and shapes and sizes! The ark held them all.

When the last animal had climbed aboard, Noah went inside and shut the door of the ark. Then the rain started to fall.

It rained and rained, and the water rose higher and higher, covering everything on Earth.

Even the tops of the highest mountains were underwater!

But the ark floated on the water and, inside, everyone was safe and warm and dry.

Finally, after forty days and forty nights, the rain stopped. Then strong winds began to blow, drying up the water. Soon the mountaintops appeared, and the ark came to rest on a mountain called Ararat.

One day Noah sent a raven out of the ark. Soon it came back—it hadn't found anywhere to land.

A week later, Noah sent a dove out.

This time it came back with an olive branch in its beak, so Noah knew that it had found some trees, and that the Earth was almost dry.

Noah waited another week, then sent the dove out again. This time the dove did not come back—it had found a place to land!

"It is time to leave the ark!" Noah told his family. He opened the doors, and all the animals went out—all the birds and beasts, and all the creeping, crawling creatures. They spread out to find homes and raise their families.

Finally, Noah and his family left the ark. They were so happy to be back on dry land!

The first thing Noah did was pray to God to say thank you for keeping him and his family safe from the flood.

Suddenly Noah saw something beautiful in the sky—a bright, shining rainbow!

"This rainbow is a sign of my promise to you, Noah," God said. "I will never again send a flood to destroy the Earth."

These days, whenever we see a rainbow in the sky, we remember Noah, and God's promise to him—and to us.

The Elves and the Shoemaker

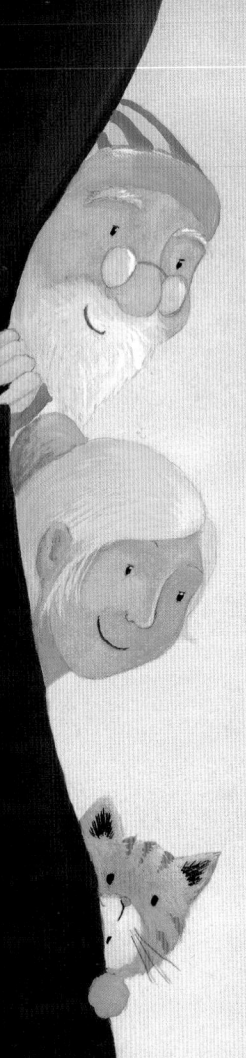

There was once a poor shoemaker who lived with his wife. "We only have enough leather to make one more pair of shoes to sell," said the shoemaker.

So he cut out the leather, ready to stitch the next day, then went to bed.

That night, two elves crept into the store, dressed in rags. They found the leather and set to work.

The next morning, the shoemaker was amazed to find the finest pair of shoes he had ever seen.

A rich gentleman saw the stylish shoes in the store and tried them on. He was so delighted with the fit that he paid the shoemaker twice the asking price.

"We can buy more leather," the shoemaker told his wife.

That evening, the shoemaker cut out two more pairs of shoes from the leather, and went to bed.

During the night, the two elves crept into the store again, and set to work on the leather.

In the morning, the shoemaker found two pairs of beautiful shoes. He sold them for more money than he had ever thought possible. Now the shoemaker had enough money to make four new pairs of shoes.

"Who is helping us?" asked the shoemaker's wife.

That night, the shoemaker cut out the new leather, then he and his wife hid and waited.

It wasn't long before the two little elves appeared and set to work on the leather.

"We must repay our little helpers for their kindness," the shoemaker told his wife.

"Let's make them some fine clothes," said his wife.

So they made the elves two little pairs of trousers, two handsome coats, and two warm, woolly scarves.

That night, the shoemaker and his wife hid again and watched as the elves found their tiny outfits! They quickly dressed, then danced away happily into the night.

The shoemaker and his wife never saw the elves again. But they continued to make fine shoes and were never poor.

Thirty Days Hath September

Thirty days hath September, April, June, and November.
All the rest have thirty-one,
Except February alone,
And that has twenty-eight days clear
And twenty-nine in each leap year.

The Farmer's in His Den

The farmer's in his den,
The farmer's in his den,
Ee-i-addio!
The farmer's in his den.

This Old Man

This old man, he played one,
He played knick-knack on my drum.
With a knick-knack, paddy whack,
Give a dog a bone,
This old man came rolling home.

Repeat the rhyme, replacing "one" and "drum" with:
two—shoe, three—knee, four—door, five—hive,
six—sticks, seven—heaven, eight—gate.

Higglety, Pigglety, Pop!

Higglety, pigglety, pop!
The dog has eaten the mop,
The pig's in a hurry,
The cat's in a flurry,
Higglety, pigglety, POP!

My Favorite Chair

My favorite chair is small like me,
I sit on it to watch TV.
And sometimes when I read a book
I take my chair into a nook
And sit there while I turn the pages,
I often stay like that for ages.

Here is the Church

Here is the church,
Here is the steeple,
Look inside ...
And see all the people!

You're Too Little!

Bobby loved being the baby of the family. It was fun to play with his big brothers. The only thing that he didn't like was being left behind when his brothers went exploring.

"You're too little to come," they said each time. "Wait till you're bigger." So while they were gone, Bobby made up songs to cheer himself up.

One day, when his brothers were just about to go off exploring, Bobby's tummy started to rumble.

"I'm hungry," he said, looking around.

There were lots of leaves on the trees, but the branches were all too high. Little Bobby stretched his trunk as far as he could, but he couldn't even touch the lowest leaf. A tear rolled down Bobby's cheek.

"Oh, don't cry, Bobby!" said one of the big elephants. He felt sorry for his little brother. He looked over at the other elephants.

"Just hold on to my tail, Bobby," said one of them. "We'll take you to the tastiest food in the jungle."

Bobby stomped into the jungle with his brothers. They led him through prickly undergrowth and past sparkling watering holes. Bobby started singing, and his brothers joined in.

At last they reached a low tree, with
bright-green leaves at just the right height for a little
elephant. Bobby used his trunk to pick a bunch of them,
and pushed them into his mouth. Yum yum! When he was
full, he told his brothers all his best jokes, and they laughed
until they cried.

"Can I always come with you on your adventures?"
Bobby asked.

His brothers wrapped their trunks around him and
laughed. "Of course you can," they said. "It's much more
fun with you here!"

How the Leopard Got Its Spots

Long ago, Leopard lived on a sandy-yellow plain in Africa. Giraffes and zebras and deer lived there too. The animals were sandy-yellow all over, just like the plain itself. Leopard was sandy-yellow, too, which wasn't good for the rest of the animals because he could hide in the sandy-yellow grasses, then jump out and eat them.

After a while the other animals had had enough. They decided to move away from the sandy plain into the forest. In the forest, the sun shone through the trees, making stripy, spotty, and patchy shadows on the ground.

The animals hid themselves there, and while they hid their skins changed color, becoming stripy, spotty, and patchy too.

Meanwhile, Leopard was hungry.

"Where has everyone gone?" he asked Baboon.

"To the forest," said Baboon carelessly, "to hide from you!"

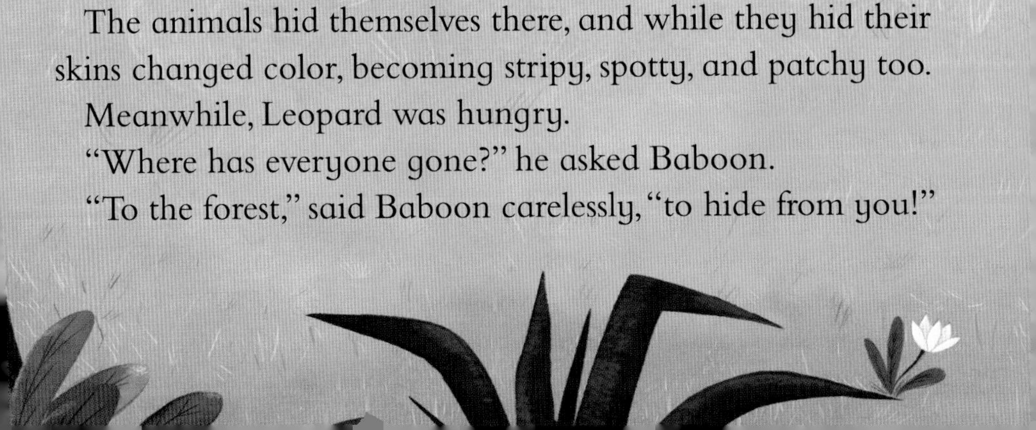

Leopard decided to go to the forest to hunt for his dinner. But when he got there, all he could see were tree trunks. They were stripy, spotty, and patchy with shadows. He couldn't see the other animals, but he could smell them so he knew they were there.

Meanwhile, the other animals could easily spot the sandy-yellow leopard in the forest, so they stayed hidden away.

Hungry and tired, Leopard lay down in a spotty shadow to rest. After a while, he noticed he wasn't sandy-yellow any more. He had small, dark spots on his skin just like the spotty shadow he was lying in.

"A-ha!" he thought. "Giraffe and Zebra and the other animals must have changed skin color too. But now my skin is no longer sandy-yellow, I can hide too. Then, when they come close, I can leap out and eat them up."

With that, the spotty leopard set off into the shadowy forest to eat, sleep and NOT be spotted. And the other animals learned to hide from him as best they could, too!

Tractor Mayhem

It was a beautiful sunny day on Friendship Farm, but Hank Hayseed couldn't enjoy it just yet. He had work to do.

"When you're finished we can have a picnic down by the duck pond," said his wife, Molly. "I'll just head into town for some groceries."

Hank and his sheepdog Gus watched Molly drive off in her old jeep.

"We'll get the chores done in no time if we use my tractor," said Hank.

Gus wasn't so sure. That tractor was pretty old! And sure enough, the moment Hank started the engine, black smoke came pouring out.

"Oh, boy!" said Hank. "What am I going to do now?"

Then he had a crackerjack idea. Hank pushed the tractor into his workshop, closed the doors, and set to work. The farm animals gathered around, trying to peek in and see what he was doing.

"Every time he tries to fix something, he only makes it worse," clucked Mrs. Beak.

"Here he comes," said Gus. "Let's skedaddle!"

Hank rode out on his tractor. "Yee-harr!" he hollered, waving his hat like a cowboy at a rodeo.

The old tractor looked as good as new. Hank had fixed it up, given it a lick of paint—and fitted rocket boosters!

"With a vehicle like this, we'll be the best farm in the whole county!" Hank said proudly. "Hop aboard, Gus—we've got work to do!"

Hank pulled the lever. Flames shot out of the rocket boosters and the tractor zoomed off!

Bailey the horse saw the tractor roaring toward him carrying hay for his breakfast.

"About time," he neighed. "I'm starving."

Hank pulled the lever to stop the tractor—and that's when everything started to go wrong. Instead of stopping, the tractor went faster! As it shot past, a hay bale flew off the trailer and landed—THUNK!—on Bailey's head.

"Sorry, Bailey!" Hank called back over his shoulder.

Hank wrestled with the pesky lever. But it was no use ... and now they were heading for old Maggie the cow.

"The lever's stuck fast!" Hank cried as Gus held on.

"I do believe," mooed Maggie grandly, "it is rude for anyone to move that fast."

But she moved fast enough herself when she saw the tractor was coming straight for her ... and wasn't going to stop!

Up ahead, Mrs. Beak and her ducklings were paddling on the pond. As the tractor splashed through the water, a wave sent them flying!

"We've got to stop this thing!" said Hank, grappling with the lever. He gave an almighty tug—and it came off in his hands.

"Jumping jelly beans!" Hank cried. "We're out of control!"

And that's when Molly arrived home.

"Are you okay?" she cried.

"Yes, dear!" Hank called back. "Just taking Wallow a bucket of pig food!"

Hank held up the bucket to show Molly as the tractor whizzed past her. Then they hit a bump and the bucket went flying out of his hands ... and landed on Molly's head!

"Hold on tiiiiiiiight!" yelled Hank as the tractor zoomed up the sloping roof of Wallow the pig's sty as if it were a ramp. It shot into the air ... and landed slap-bang in the middle of the duck pond!

Hank and Gus were soaked and Friendship Farm was a terrible mess.

"This'll take all day to fix!" groaned Hank.

"Nonsense!" said Molly, still pulling food scraps from her hair. "We can do it and still have time for a picnic, just as long as we all pitch in and work together!"

And everyone agreed that was a crackerjack idea.

Jack-a-Dandy

Nauty pauty Jack-a-Dandy,
Stole a piece of sugar candy
From the grocer's shoppy shop,
And away did hoppy-hop.

Tommy's Shop

Tommy kept a chandler's shop,
Richard went to buy a mop;
Tommy gave him such a whop,
That sent him out of the chandler's shop.

Simple Simon

Simple Simon met a pieman,
Going to the fair;
Said Simple Simon to the pieman,
"Let me taste your ware."

Said the pieman to Simple Simon,
"Show me first your penny."
Said Simple Simon to the pieman,
"Indeed I have not any."

Tommy Snooks and Bessy Brooks

As Tommy Snooks and Bessy Brooks
Were walking out one Sunday,
Says Tommy Snooks to Bessy Brooks,
"Tomorrow will be Monday."

Billy Booster

Billy Billy Booster,
Had a little rooster,
The rooster died,
And Billy cried.
Poor Billy Booster.

Peter, Peter, Pumpkin Eater

Peter, Peter, pumpkin eater,
Had a wife and couldn't keep her;
He put her in a pumpkin shell
And there he kept her very well.

Want to Swap?

It was bedtime, but Duck couldn't sleep. "I'm bored with being a duck and nibbling waterweeds," she said to herself.

Then she saw her friend Cockerel strolling around the pond and had a bright idea.

"Hey, Cockerel," she called. "Want to swap jobs?"

"Okay," Cockerel agreed. "Nibbling waterweeds is better than getting up early every day."

So the next morning, Duck waddled to the farmhouse for her first cock-a-doodle-do to wake the farmer up. But when she opened her beak ...

"Quack! Quack! QUACK!"

Poor Duck! However hard she tried, she couldn't crow, and the farmer overslept.

"I want my old job back," Duck said sadly.

Luckily for Duck, Cockerel was not enjoying his new job much either.

"Waterweeds are yucky and I kind of missed waking the farmer up," he said.

The next day, when Duck saw Sheepdog herding sheep, she had a thought. She waddled up to the field.

"That looks like fun, Sheepdog," she said. "Want to swap?"

Sheep's Bad Mood

Sheep was in a bad mood. His friends on the farm tried to cheer him up, but their jokes didn't help. Sheep just felt as if there were a growly bear inside him trying to get out.

"I've an idea," said Horse, who was very clever about this sort of thing. "Try doing some hard work."

"How can hard work help?" Sheep grumbled. But no one had any better ideas, so Sheep decided to give it a try. He carried baskets of eggs for the chickens. He lifted bales of hay for the horses. He rode in the tractor with the farmer. He worked so hard that he started to forget about his bad mood. And at bedtime, when all the weary farm animals snuggled down in the barn, Horse noticed that Sheep was smiling.

"Has it gone?" asked Horse.

"Has what gone?" yawned Sheep.

"Your bad mood," said Horse, chuckling loudly.

But there was no reply. Sheep was already fast asleep!

The Princes and the Water Sprite

Once upon a time there lived a king who had three sons. The Star Prince and the Moon Prince were the sons of his first wife, and his youngest son, the Sun Prince, was the son of his second wife. When his youngest son was born, he promised to give the second queen any gift she wanted.

Many years later, when the three princes were grown up, the second queen asked the king for her gift. She wanted him to hand over the kingdom to her son.

"I can't do that, my dear," cried the king. "It is the custom for the kingdom to go to the eldest son. Please ask for something else."

The queen was cross and the king worried that she might try to harm the elder princes. So, with a heavy heart, he sent them off to live in the forest, until the Star Prince could return and rule.

The youngest son loved his older brothers and decided to leave with them. Soon they came to a pond. The pond belonged to a water sprite. He had the power to enslave anyone who came to drink from the pond and failed to give the correct answer to his question.

128

The Sun Prince went to fetch some water. When the water sprite saw him, he asked, "What are the good fairies like?"

The Sun Prince replied, "They are like the sun and the moon."

"No!" cried the sprite and took the youngest prince to his cave. When he didn't return, the Moon Prince went to look for him.

"O, Prince, what are the good fairies like?" asked the sprite.

"They are like the sky above us," replied the Moon Prince.

"No!" screeched the sprite, and took him to his cave.

When the Star Prince came to look for his younger brothers, the sprite asked him the same question.

"If I get the answer right, you must return my brothers," demanded the Star Prince. "The good fairies are pure in heart and kindly in word and deed."

The sprite was so pleased with the prince's answer that he released the brothers from captivity.

The brothers lived happily together in the forest. When the queen died, they returned together to the city, where the Star Prince became a wise and kind ruler.

Sleepysaurus

Mommysaurus smiled at her son and cuddled him close. Sleepysaurus' eyes were starting to droop.

"Come on sleepyhead!" she laughed. "It's time for bed."

But Sleepysaurus didn't want to go to bed.

"Bed's boring! I don't want to go to sleep. Sleep's boring! I want to have another story!"

"You're yawning," Mommysaurus said, gently tucking him into bed. "That shows how tired you are."

"Yawns are boring!"

Sleepysaurus' mouth opened wider ... and wider ... but, just in time, he turned the yawn into a ...

ROAR!

"What's all this noise?" said Daddysaurus, rushing in.

"It's Sleepysaurus," said Mommysaurus. "He won't go to sleep. He won't even let himself yawn!"

Daddysaurus smiled and read Sleepysaurus another story. And another ... and another ... and another!

Sleepysaurus felt an even bigger yawn coming on. His mouth opened wider and wider, but he turned it into a ...

ROAR!

"I've got an idea, Sleepysaurus! Let's go for a walk. Maybe that'll tire you out," said Daddysaurus.

"Look at the beautiful stars," Daddysaurus said, when they stepped outside their cave. "Why don't you count them!"

"One, two, three ..." counted Sleepysaurus. By the time he'd got to fifty-six, he felt the most enormous yawn coming on.

His mouth opened wider and wider, but he turned it into a ...

ROAR!

The sound echoed through the stillness of the night, getting louder and louder and louder ...

But it wasn't an echo! It was a very big, very angry ... T. Rex! And it was running toward them!

"Who's that waking me up?" roared the T. Rex.

Daddysaurus grabbed Sleepysaurus and raced, top speed, all the way home ...

"Roars are boring," said Sleepysaurus. "I think I'll go to bed now."

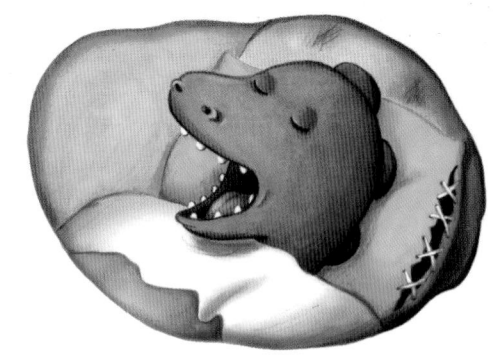

As Sleepysaurus climbed into bed he felt the most ginormous yawn coming on. His mouth opened wider and wider and ...

YAWN!

ZZZZzz!

Row, Row, Row Your Boat

Row, row, row your boat,
Gently down the stream,
Merrily, merrily, merrily, merrily,
Life is but a dream.

Jay-bird

Jay-bird, jay-bird, sittin' on a rail,
Pickin' his teeth with the end of his tail;
Mulberry leaves and calico sleeves—
All schoolteachers are hard to please.

Spin, Dame

Spin, dame, spin,
Your bread you must win;
Twist the thread and break it not,
Spin, dame, spin.

The Robin and the Wren

The robin and the wren,
They fought upon the porridge pan;
But before the robin got a spoon,
The wren had eaten the porridge down.

The Mouse's Lullaby

Oh, rock-a-bye, baby mouse, rock-a-bye, so!
When baby's asleep to the baker's I'll go,
And while he's not looking I'll pop from a hole,
And bring to my baby a fresh penny roll.

Bow-wow

Bow-wow, says the dog,
Mew, mew, says the cat,
Grunt, grunt, goes the hog,
And squeak goes the rat.
Tu-whu, says the owl,
Caw, caw, says the crow,
Quack, quack, says the duck,
And what cuckoos say you know.

The Best Cuddle Ever!

Arthur Bear and his friend Ben usually loved splashing in the forest pool. But today, Arthur didn't jump into the water with Ben. He didn't feel very well.

"What do you need?" asked Ben, clambering out of the pool and shaking the water off his fur. "Medicine? Ointment?"

"No, I need a cuddle," Arthur said. But what sort of cuddle should it be? He just couldn't decide.

"How about a friend cuddle?" Ben asked, wrapping his arms around Arthur and squeezing him.

"Brrr, no, that's too damp," said Arthur with a shiver. Arthur tried giving the holly bush a hug, but that was much too prickly.

Arthur set off for home, and on the way he saw a little hedgehog. "How sweet!" he said, but the hedgehog's cuddle was much too spiky.

He got a cuddle from a spider, but that was too tickly. His friend the snake's cuddle was too squeezy.

"Nothing can make me feel better," he said, sitting down. His eyes closed. Then two big arms went around him and lifted him into the air.

Warm fur was all around him. Someone big was carrying him to bed.

"Daddy," Arthur whispered. "Now I feel better." His father tucked him in and snuggled up next to him. A daddy cuddle was exactly what Arthur had needed!

Ride a Cock Horse

Ride a cock horse to Banbury Cross
To see a fine lady upon a white horse.
With rings on her fingers and bells on her toes,
She shall have music wherever she goes.

Mary Had a Little Lamb

Mary had a little lamb,
Its fleece was white as snow,
And everywhere that Mary went
The lamb was sure to go.
It followed her to school one day,
Which was against the rule.
It made the children laugh and play
To see a lamb at school.

See a Pin

See a pin and pick it up,
All the day you'll have good luck;
See a pin and let it lay,
Bad luck you'll have all the day!

I Eat My Peas
with Honey

I eat my peas with honey,
I've done it all my life,
It makes the peas taste funny,
But it keeps them on my knife.

Little Miss Muffet

Little Miss Muffet
Sat on a tuffet,
Eating her curds and whey.
Along came a spider,
Who sat down beside her
And frightened Miss Muffet away!

Don't Be Scared

Dad put his arm around Little Cub. "I think the time's right for you to come out with me to explore tonight."

Little Cub peered at the evening sky. The sun was slipping down behind the trees. Shadows stretched across the plain.

As they set off, Little Cub shivered, and suddenly stopped.

"What's that high up there in that tree?" he asked. "There are two great big eyes watching me."

"Look closer, Little Cub. That thing up there is just old Owl. Did he give you a scare?" asked Dad.

"Dad," smiled Little Cub, "Owl won't give me a scare. He can't do that, as long as you're there."

Suddenly, Little Cub stopped. "What's that black shape hanging down from that tree? I felt it reaching out for me."

"Look closer, Little Cub. That thing up there is just old Snake. Did he give you a scare?" asked Dad.

"Dad," smiled Little Cub, "Snake won't give me a scare. He can't do that, as long as you're there."

Dad and Little Cub walked on. Suddenly, Little Cub stopped.

"What's that I can hear
behind that tree? There's
a huge black shadow following us."

"Look closer, Little Cub. That thing
back there is just old Elephant. Did he give you
a scare?" asked Dad.

"Dad," smiled Little Cub, "Elephant won't give me a scare.
He can't do that, as long as you're there."

Dad and Little Cub walked on. Suddenly, Dad stopped.

"What's that?" he asked.

"Hooo, hooooo! Sssss, Sssss! Terummmp, terummmp!"

The animals jumped out at Dad. Dad jumped!

"Don't be scared," laughed Little Cub.

"Sorry, Lion! Did we give you a fright?" asked the animals,
laughing.

"No!" said Dad, smiling. "You couldn't give me a scare.
Not as long as Little Cub is there."

Then, side by side, Little Cub and Dad headed for home.

The Wolf in Sheep's Clothing

Night after night, a hungry wolf prowled around a flock of sheep, looking for one he could eat, but the shepherd always spotted him and chased him away.

One night, when the wolf was on the point of giving up, he found an old sheepskin that the shepherd had thrown aside. Grinning, the wolf pulled the skin carefully over himself so that none of his fur showed under the woolly fleece. Then he slowly strolled into the middle of the flock.

After a while, a lamb came up to the wolf. Thinking the wolf was its mother the lamb followed the wolf into the woods. Poor little lamb! The hungry wolf gobbled it up!

On the following night, and for several nights after that, the cunning wolf used his clever disguise, feasting on the sheep whenever he pleased.

And the moral of this story is: Things are not always as they appear to be.

The Man, the Bird and the Ogres

One day a man went into the forest to cut wood. He worked hard all day and was about to set off home when he saw a sickly bird, quivering on the path in front of him. He stopped to give it some food and water.

"You have been so kind," chirped the bird. "One day I will help you too."

The man smiled, but he didn't really believe that such a tiny creature could help him.

Several weeks later, when the man was in the forest again, four huge ogres came running toward him through the trees. He was terrified. He scrambled up a tree to hide. Suddenly, a little bird appeared. It started singing sweetly, while flying from tree to tree. The singing distracted the ogres and they started following the delightful sound.

The man quietly slid down the tree and ran all the way home. The little bird he once helped had now saved him from the ogres.

Why the Sea is Salty

Once upon a time there were two brothers, one rich and one poor. The day came when the poor brother had no food left in his house and so he went to his rich brother to beg him for something to eat.

The rich brother was not happy about this, but he said, "I will give you this ham, but you must go straight to Dead Man's Hall with it."

The poor brother was so grateful for the food that he agreed to do as the rich brother asked.

He walked and walked all day. It was just getting dark when he came to a large building. There was an old man outside, chopping wood.

"Excuse me, kind sir," said the brother. "I am going to Dead Man's Hall. Am I on the right track?"

"Oh, yes!" replied the old man. "You are here. When you go inside, the people there will want to buy your ham. Don't sell it to them unless they give you the hand-mill which stands behind the door."

The poor brother thanked the old man for his advice, and went into the hall. Everything happened just as the old man had said it would. The poor brother left the hall with the hand-mill. He asked the old man how it worked and then set off home.

Now the hand-mill was magic. When the poor brother got home, he asked it to grind a feast of food and drink for himself and his wife. To stop the hand-mill the poor brother simply needed to say, "Thank you, magic mill, you can stop now."

When the rich brother saw that his brother was no longer poor, he became jealous and angry.

"Give me that mill," he insisted when he saw what it could do. The brother had everything he needed, so he sold the mill to his rich brother, but he did not tell him how to stop it grinding.

When the rich brother got the mill home, he immediately asked it to grind lots of food. But because he didn't know how to stop it, the mill carried on grinding food until it was flowing out of the house and across the fields. He ran to his brother's house.

"Please take it back!" he cried. "If it doesn't stop grinding soon the whole town will be destroyed."

So the brother took it back, and was never poor or hungry again.

Soon the story of the wonderful magic mill spread far and wide.

One day a merchant sailor knocked at the brother's door.

"Does the mill grind salt?" he asked.

"Of course," replied the brother. "It will grind whatever you ask."

The sailor was desperate to have the mill so that he wouldn't have to sail far away over the perilous sea to buy the bags of salt he bought and sold.

"I will give you a thousand coins for the mill," cried the sailor.

At first the brother was reluctant to sell it, but then he decided that he had gained more than enough from it, so he agreed.

The sailor was in such a hurry to leave and try the mill out, that he forgot to ask the brother how to stop it grinding. When he had gone a little way out to sea, he put the mill on deck and said, "Grind salt, and grind both quickly and well."

Of course, the mill did his bidding, but it didn't stop. The heap of salt grew bigger and bigger, until at last the ship sank under the weight of it.

The mill still lies at the bottom of the sea to this day. And day by day, it grinds on and on, and that is why the sea is salty.

The Rainbow's End

How did it get there, so pretty and bright?
It must be a magical fairy light.
Shimmering colors, up so high,
A beautiful rainbow, painting the sky!

Is it a wonderful fairyland slide,
Where pixies and fairies can go for a ride?
I'd like to follow it, because I'm told
At the rainbow's end is a pot of gold!

Itsy Bitsy Spider

Itsy Bitsy Spider
Climbing up the spout.
Down came the rain
And washed the spider out.

Out came the sun
And dried up all the rain.
Itsy Bitsy Spider
Climbed up the spout again.

Giddy Up, Teddy

Giddy up, Teddy,
Don't you stop!
Ride on the hobbyhorse,
Clippety clop!
Clippety clopping,
Round and round,
Giddy up,
We're toybox bound!

Round and Round the Garden

Round and round the garden
Like a teddy bear.
One step, two steps,
Tickly under there!

Here We Go Round the Mulberry Bush

Here we go round the mulberry bush,
The mulberry bush, the mulberry bush,
Here we go round the mulberry bush,
On a cold and frosty morning.

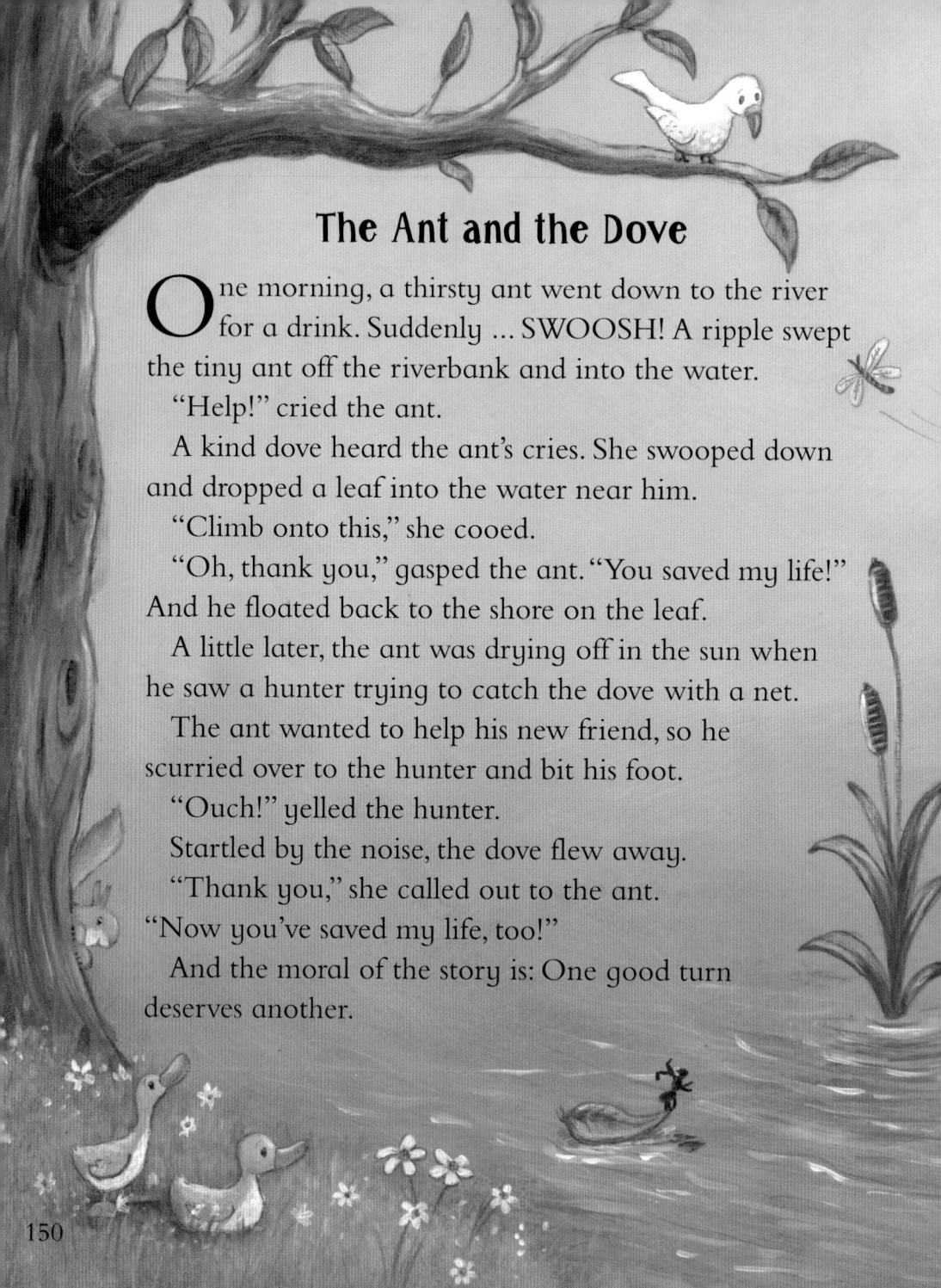

The Ant and the Dove

One morning, a thirsty ant went down to the river for a drink. Suddenly ... SWOOSH! A ripple swept the tiny ant off the riverbank and into the water.

"Help!" cried the ant.

A kind dove heard the ant's cries. She swooped down and dropped a leaf into the water near him.

"Climb onto this," she cooed.

"Oh, thank you," gasped the ant. "You saved my life!" And he floated back to the shore on the leaf.

A little later, the ant was drying off in the sun when he saw a hunter trying to catch the dove with a net.

The ant wanted to help his new friend, so he scurried over to the hunter and bit his foot.

"Ouch!" yelled the hunter.

Startled by the noise, the dove flew away.

"Thank you," she called out to the ant. "Now you've saved my life, too!"

And the moral of the story is: One good turn deserves another.

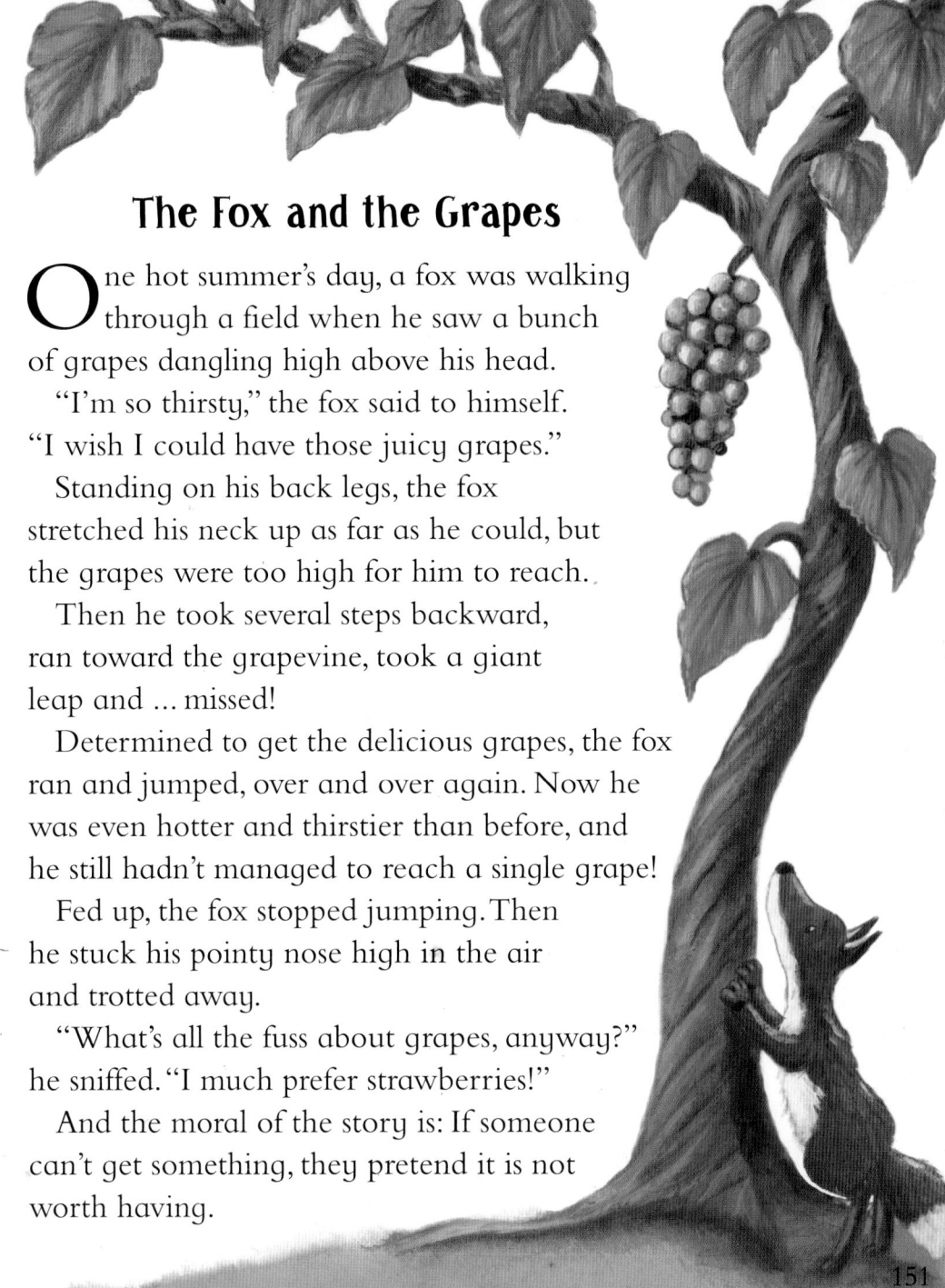

The Fox and the Grapes

One hot summer's day, a fox was walking through a field when he saw a bunch of grapes dangling high above his head.

"I'm so thirsty," the fox said to himself. "I wish I could have those juicy grapes."

Standing on his back legs, the fox stretched his neck up as far as he could, but the grapes were too high for him to reach.

Then he took several steps backward, ran toward the grapevine, took a giant leap and ... missed!

Determined to get the delicious grapes, the fox ran and jumped, over and over again. Now he was even hotter and thirstier than before, and he still hadn't managed to reach a single grape!

Fed up, the fox stopped jumping. Then he stuck his pointy nose high in the air and trotted away.

"What's all the fuss about grapes, anyway?" he sniffed. "I much prefer strawberries!"

And the moral of the story is: If someone can't get something, they pretend it is not worth having.

Alex and the Egyptian Magic

So far, Alex wasn't enjoying Egypt very much. "You can write about the pyramids in your vacation report," said his mom. But Alex didn't think the pyramids or the guide were very interesting.

"This pyramid was built as a tomb for a mummified Egyptian pharaoh king," the guide explained. "A special ancient magic keeps his tomb hidden, even though hundreds of people have looked for his treasure."

"I don't believe that," said Alex. Just then he spotted a tiny door in the side of the pyramid. While his parents weren't looking, he opened the door and crept inside. He found a long tunnel with hieroglyphics on the wall. Alex's heart thumped with excitement. At last something fun was happening!

He crawled along the tunnel until it opened out into a big chamber lit with flaming torches. He saw a mummy wrapped in white bandages, surrounded by glittering treasures. Golden goblets, necklaces, bowls, and statues sparkled with rubies and emeralds.

"I've found the mummy's treasure!" Alex exclaimed. But as soon as his finger touched a golden lamp, WHOOSH! Something yanked him out of the chamber and back to his parents and the tour guide.

Alex looked around in confusion. The little door had disappeared. "Are you all right?" asked his mom.

Alex tried to explain, but to his surprise he said, "Fine thanks." Something was stopping him from talking about the chamber! He looked at the guide, who simply winked.

"As I said," the guide went on, "the ancient magic won't let anyone reveal the king's tomb."

Alex smiled. Even though he wouldn't be able to write about it in his vacation report, he would never forget the thrill of discovering the secret chamber and the mummy's treasure.

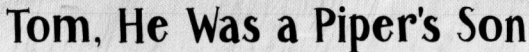

Tom, He Was a Piper's Son

Tom, he was a piper's son,
He learnt to play when he was young,
And the only tune that he could play,
Was, "Over the hills and far away".
Over the hills and a great way off,
The wind shall blow my top knot off!

Old John Muddlecombe

Old John Muddlecombe lost his cap,
He couldn't find it anywhere, the poor old chap.
He walked down the High Street, and everybody said,
"Silly John Muddlecombe, you've got it on your head!"

Robert Rowley

Robert Rowley rolled a round roll 'round,
A round roll Robert Rowley rolled 'round;
Where rolled the round roll
Robert Rowley rolled 'round?

154

Jack and Guy

Jack and Guy went out in the rye.
And they found a little boy with one black eye.
Come, says Jack, let's knock him on the head,
No, says Guy, let's buy him some bread;
You buy one loaf and I'll buy two,
And we'll bring him up as other folk do.

Peter Piper

Peter Piper picked a peck of pickled peppers;
A peck of pickled peppers Peter Piper picked;
If Peter Piper picked a peck of pickled peppers,
Where's the peck of pickled peppers Peter Piper picked?

Old Joe Brown

Old Joe Brown, he had a wife,
She was all of eight feet tall.
She slept with her head in the kitchen,
And her feet stuck out in the hall.

Little Chief Bear!

The brown bears lived beside the river. Every spring, they had a fishing competition. Each bear stood on a rock in the river and waited. Soon the fish would start to splash, and then the bears would use their paws to flip the fish out of the water. Whoever caught the most fish was the winner, and the winner got a wonderful prize. He or she was declared Chief Bear for the whole year.

Alex was the very smallest bear of all. He was too short to climb the big trees. He was too little to wade in the deepest part of the river. But Alex had big, BIG dreams.

"I want to win the fishing competition," he said. "I want to change things for little bears like me. None of the big bears think we are important. I want them to know that we matter too."

Everyone laughed when Alex joined the competition. "You're too little to be a good fisher," said one of the bigger bears. "You're too little to be good at anything!"

Even the Chief Bear laughed at him. "Leave the fishing to the big bears," he said. "Go and play with the other babies."

But Alex put his chin up and stepped onto a rock in the middle of the river. The other bears laughed again.

"He'll never win," they said, shaking their heads. "He should just give up."

Alex didn't say anything. He just peered into the water, looking for fish. There was a silvery flash and he splashed his paw into the water.

"Missed," said one of the biggest bears, chuckling. "You had better give up."

Alex just put his head down and looked into the water again. This time he didn't try to catch the fish. He just watched. And after a few minutes of standing completely still, he noticed something. The fish were clever! They could see the bears that were splashing around in the water, and they were trying to swim away from danger. But they didn't realize that Alex was a bear too, because he was standing so still, and they were swimming straight toward him.

Flick! One fish landed on the rock beside Alex. Flick! Flick! His paw moved so fast that the fish didn't see him coming. His pile of fish grew larger and larger and larger. The minutes went by, and at last the Chief Bear held up his paw.

"Stop!" he said. "The competition is over. Now it's time to count the fish."

When all the fish had been counted, the Chief Bear's mouth fell open in surprise. Then he climbed onto a log and looked around at all the bears.

"We have all been very silly," he said. "We thought that because Alex was small, he wasn't as good as us. But Alex is better than us. He has won the competition! Alex is our new Chief Bear."

He stepped down from the log, and
Alex stepped up to take his place. He
couldn't see very well, so he stood up
on his hind legs.

"I will try to be a good Chief," he said.
"And my first command is that all bears,
big and small, must be treated equally,
because they are all just as important
as each other!"

The Boy Who Wanted More Cheese

Klaas was a young Dutch boy, who lived with his family on a farm. There was always plenty to eat—wonderful breads, potatoes, and Klaas' favorite, cheese. Klaas loved cheese more than any other food. At meal times he would always try and get his sisters to give him their portions, until his mother scolded him.

"Klaas, you are going to burst if you eat any more cheese," she cried.

Even when his stomach was full, Klass still wanted more cheese. He was a good boy in all other ways, but his love of cheese always led him into trouble.

One night when he had been sent to bed early for taking his sisters' cheese again, Klaas lay sulking on his bed, looking out of his window.

Suddenly, he saw little lights moving around a tree in the garden, and he heard a tiny, tinkling voice.

"There's plenty of cheese. Come with us."

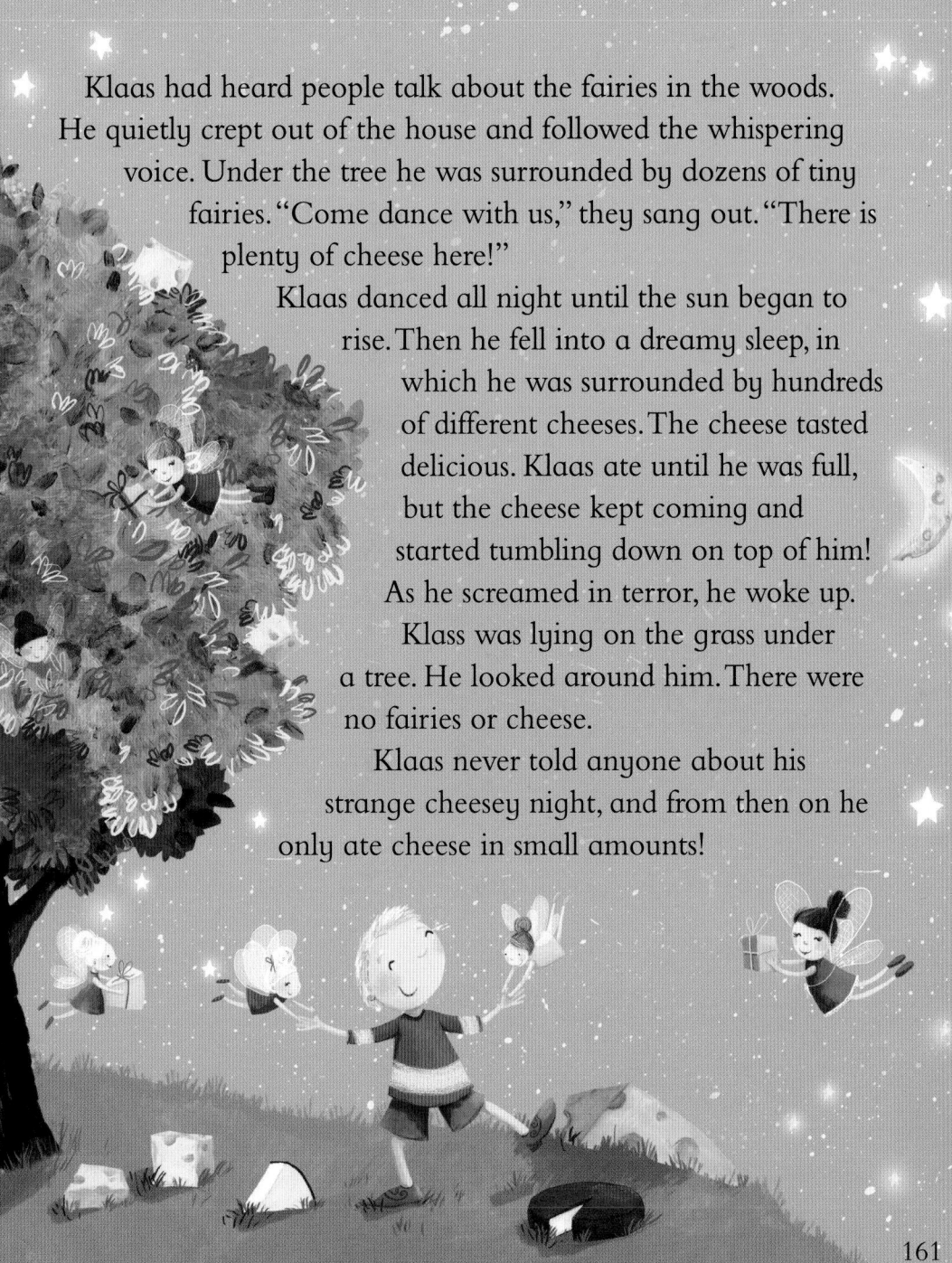

Klaas had heard people talk about the fairies in the woods. He quietly crept out of the house and followed the whispering voice. Under the tree he was surrounded by dozens of tiny fairies. "Come dance with us," they sang out. "There is plenty of cheese here!"

Klaas danced all night until the sun began to rise. Then he fell into a dreamy sleep, in which he was surrounded by hundreds of different cheeses. The cheese tasted delicious. Klaas ate until he was full, but the cheese kept coming and started tumbling down on top of him! As he screamed in terror, he woke up. Klass was lying on the grass under a tree. He looked around him. There were no fairies or cheese.

Klaas never told anyone about his strange cheesey night, and from then on he only ate cheese in small amounts!

Jack Be Nimble

Jack be nimble,
And Jack be quick:
And Jack jump over
The candlestick.

The Man in the Wilderness

The man in the wilderness asked me,
How many strawberries grew in the sea?
I answered him as I thought good,
As many red herrings as grew in the wood.

Fire on the Mountain

Rats in the garden—catch 'em Towser!
Cows in the cornfield—run boys run!
Cat's in the cream pot—stop her now, sir!
Fire on the mountain—run boys run!

If All the World Was Apple-pie

If all the world was apple-pie,
And all the sea was ink,
And all the trees were bread and cheese,
What should we have for drink?

This Little Piggy

This little piggy went to market,
This little piggy stayed at home,
This little piggy had roast beef,
This little piggy had none,
And this little piggy cried
Wee-wee-wee-wee-wee!
All the way home.

Bob Robin

Little Bob Robin,
Where do you live?
Up in yonder wood, sir,
On a hazel twig.

Silly Billy

Bats do a lot of things upside down. They eat upside down. They sleep upside down. But Billy Bat spent so much time upside down that he thought up was down!

One night, Billy saw the reflection of the moon in the lake as he hung from his perch.

"I want to fly to the moon," he said.

"Don't be silly, Billy," said his sister, Grace. "The moon is too far away."

"No it's not," said Billy, pointing to the reflection. "It's really close—look!"

Grace shook her head. "You don't understand!" she said.

But Billy wasn't listening.

"Here I go!" he cried. "Wheeee!" He spread his wings and zoomed toward the reflection of the moon in the water. SPLASH! Billy dived into the lake. A few seconds later he crawled out, spluttering, and found his sister waiting for him.

"Do you understand now, Billy?" Grace asked.

"Yes," said Billy, shivering. "The moon is much, much wetter than it looks!"

What a silly Billy!

Fluff's Muddle

Fluff was all in a muddle. During the daytime, when owls should be asleep, Fluff was wide awake. There was just so much happening on the farm! She giggled at the geese waddling around the pond and chuckled as the chickens scratched and pecked the ground. She laughed so much that she kept waking her family up.

"You're too noisy," said her sister, Blink.

"You're keeping us awake!" said her brother, Beak.

That night, Fluff was feeling tired, just when owls should be wide awake.

"I know what we can do to fix Fluff's muddle," said Blink.

Fluff could hardly believe her eyes as Blink and Beak waddled round the pond like geese, and scratched and pecked the ground like chickens. She laughed so much that it kept her awake all night.

By the time morning came, Fluff was feeling very tired indeed. The geese waddled and the chickens scratched and pecked as usual, but Fluff was fast asleep.

The Tin Soldier

Once there was a little boy who lived in a townhouse at the end of a leafy avenue. It was a very happy home.

On the boy's birthday there were balloons, a magnificent cake, and a small pile of colorfully wrapped presents. The boy undid the ribbon and pulled back the paper on the first package, his eyes glittering with excitement.

"Tin soldiers!" cried the boy, as he opened his present. "Thank you, Mom and Dad. I love them!"

He lined them up along his playroom floor. When he got to the last soldier in the box, he paused.

"Oh!" he said. "This soldier has only one leg."

The soldiers had been made from some old tin spoons and there hadn't been quite enough metal to finish the last man. Despite missing a leg, the tin soldier stood upright and steady.

"This one must go on parade, too," decided the boy. "He is just as neat and brave as the others."

The boy spent the rest of his birthday evening playing with his new toys. At the other end of the playroom there was a fine wooden castle.

When the boy carried the tin soldier with one leg past the toy castle, something caught the soldier's eye. There, in the doorway, was a beautiful paper doll ballerina. She stood on one leg, with her other leg pointed out behind her.

"She stands on one leg, just as I do," marveled the soldier. "What a wonderful wife she would make!"

Soon the boy left the room to go to bed. The tin soldier hid behind a box on the windowsill. From his hiding place, he gazed at the ballerina all night. In her castle, the ballerina was frozen too, fixed in her pose. The soldier and the dancer stared into each other's eyes all night long, not turning away for a moment.

When morning came, a maid came in to tidy the room. As she opened the window, she accidentally knocked the tin soldier over the ledge.

Down, down, down, the soldier fell, dropping at last into a drain in the street below.

"Stand tall, soldier! Bravely meet your fate!" he cried, as he was washed through dark pipes and out into a river.

As the tin soldier sank down into the murky waters of the river, he thought of the beautiful ballerina to give him courage. Suddenly, everything went dark. The soldier had been swallowed by a big blue fish.

The fish twisted and turned in the water. But just when the soldier was certain that he would be crushed to death, the creature became still. The soldier stayed still, as light burst into the darkness. The fish had been caught and cut open and was lying in a kitchen, ready to be cooked.

"Oh, good heavens!" cried a voice. "Our lost soldier!"

By a stroke of good luck, the soldier had come back to the house of the little boy. The cook washed him and gave him to the maid to put back in the boy's playroom.

The soldier's heart burst with joy. He was near to his beloved ballerina once again.

The next day, however, as the boy played, he accidentally knocked the tin soldier into the fire.

"No!" cried the boy. But it was too late. The tin soldier had already started to melt away.

Suddenly, a gust of wind curled in through the open window, lifting the ballerina off her feet. She twirled once before disappearing into the flames beside the soldier. At the same time, the tin soldier melted into the coals, bound together forever with the ashes of his beautiful ballerina.

Jack's School Trip

Jack yawned and rubbed his eyes. He was so excited he had hardly slept. The day of the class trip to the Space Center had finally come!

As soon as they arrived, Jack's class was taken on a tour. They visited Mission Control, saw astronauts in training and touched a real space rock. Then, best of all, they were allowed to step on board a rocket.

"Time for lunch, children," said Miss Jones, their teacher. All the pupils filed out of the rocket with Jack dawdling at the back. He just wanted to have one last look at the controls.

"3 ... 2 ... 1 ... BLASTOFF!" he whispered as he sat down in one of the atronaut's seats.

Suddenly, the door clanged shut. There was an earsplitting roar and the ground shook.

"Uh-oh!" said Jack. Then he was whooshing into the air, faster than he had ever traveled. Jack was heading straight into space!

He floated upside down and looked out of the window. He could see the moon, the Earth, and lots of stars. Then he saw a flying saucer!

Green aliens with three eyes waved to him.

Jack gulped and sat at the controls, trying to remember everything he had read about rockets. Then he pressed a large red button and crossed his fingers.

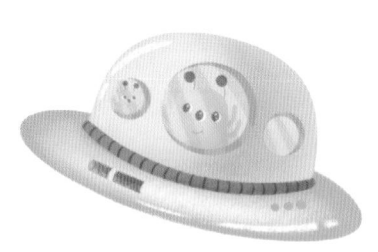

WHOOOSH! The rocket turned and hurtled back toward Earth at top speed.

"Yikes!" cried Jack. "I'm going to crash!" He squeezed his eyes shut and prepared for landing.

"Earth calling Jack!" came a voice. Jack opened his eyes to see Miss Jones standing over him with a stern look on his face. He had fallen asleep in the rocket and dreamed the whole thing. "Phew!" grinned Jack. "It's good to be back!"

Down With the Lambs

Down with the lambs,
Up with the lark,
Run to bed, children,
Before it gets dark.

Brown Bird

Little brown bird,
Where do you live?
"Up in yonder wood, sir,
On a hazel twig."

Gee Up, Horsey

Gee up, horsey, off we go,
Clippety cloppety, nice and slow.
Clippety, cloppety, down the lane,
All the way, then back again.

Feathers

Cackle, cackle, Mother Goose,
Have you any feathers loose?
"Truly have I, pretty fellow,
Half enough to fill a pillow.
Here are quills, take one or two,
And down to make a bed for you."

A Green Frog

Said the little green frog,
As he sat on a log,
"Nobody really likes me."
A duck came along,
And said, "You are wrong"
And gobbled him up for tea.

An Elephant Walks

An elephant walks like this and that;
He's terribly tall and he's terribly fat.
He's got no fingers,
He's got no toes,
But goodness gracious
What a long, long nose!

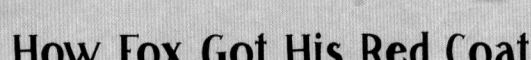

How Fox Got His Red Coat

Long ago, an old widow woman grew vegetables in her small garden, and sold them to make her living.

The woman worked very hard every day, tending her plants, so she was upset to discover that someone had been stealing some of her cabbages in the night. That someone was the wily Rabbit.

The next night the old woman set a clever trap and caught Rabbit. She tied him up in a sack.

While Rabbit was lying in the sack wondering how he was going to escape, a sleek, black fox came prowling along. He didn't see the sack in the dark, and tripped over it.

"What are you doing, hiding in a sack?" asked Fox.

Rabbit quickly thought of a plan. "The woman who owns this garden wants me to marry her granddaughter," he replied. "When I refused she caught me. She's gone to get the girl now."

"I've been looking for a wife for a long time," said the Fox. "I'll marry her. Let me swap places with you."

Fox untied the sack, let Rabbit out, and got in it himself. Rabbit tied it back up and hurried away as quickly as he could.

The old woman came back. "I will stop you now, thief!"

When Fox heard these words, he knew Rabbit had tricked him. As soon as the woman opened the sack he sprang out before she could catch him.

Fox was angry at being tricked. He wanted revenge!

Fox found Rabbit sitting on a stone playing his flute.

"What are you doing?" he asked.

"I'm practicing for a wedding," replied Rabbit. "They're going to pay me handsomely. Why don't you join me and share the money."

Fox was a greedy fellow, and he thought he'd get the money and then steal the rest from Rabbit.

"I don't have a flute," he said to Rabbit.

"Don't worry, my friend," said the clever Rabbit. "I'll just head home and get my other flute for you."

Rabbit knew the Fox wanted to trick him, so he set fire to the grass around the stone and ran away.

Fox had to jump through the flames to save himself. His sleek black coat was scorched to red-brown.

He was so glad to be alive that he decided to give up on his revenge— Rabbit was far too clever for him. But since that night the Rabbit and the Fox have never been friends, and all the foxes that came after Fox have always had a red-brown coat.

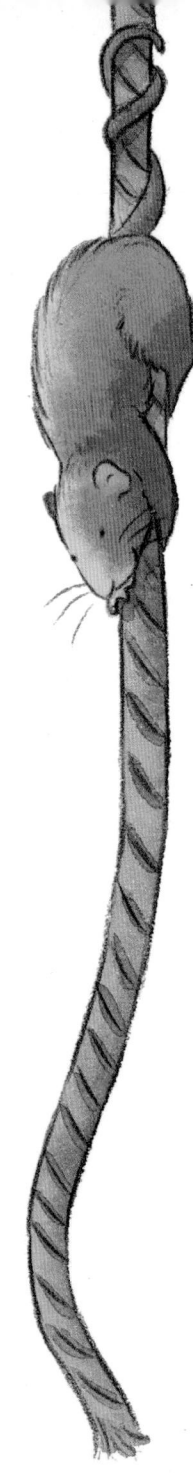

A Rat

There was a rat,
For want of stairs,
Went down a rope
To say his prayers.

Diddelty, Diddelty

Diddlety, diddlety, dumpty,
The cat ran up the plum tree;
Half a crown to fetch her down,
Diddlety, diddlety, dumpty.

Milking

Let down thy milk, old brown cow,
Let down thy milk and I'll give you a bow;
A bow, a coin, and a golden key,
If thou wilt make sweet white milk for me.

Little Jack Jingle

Little Jack Jingle,
He used to live single:
But when he got tired of this kind of life,
He left off being single, and lived with his wife.

Way Down Yonder in the Maple Swamp

Way down yonder in the maple swamp
The wild geese gather and the ganders honk;
The mares kick up and the ponies prance;
The old sow whistles and the little pigs dance.

Follow My Bangalorey Man

Follow my Bangalorey Man,
Follow my Bangalorey Man;
I'll do all that ever I can
To follow my Bangalorey Man.
We'll borrow a horse, and steal a gig,
And round the world we'll do a jig,
And I'll do all that ever I can
To follow my Bangalorey Man!

The Magic Merry-Go-Round

Danny didn't enjoy going shopping with Mom. It took much too long! She always wanted to go into every single store downtown. They had already been into the butcher's, the cheese store, the clothes store and the shoe store. The only store they hadn't gone into was the toy store. They had met nine of Mom's friends, and she had spent much too long talking to them.

"I just want to stop at the grocer's," said Mom. Danny was about to groan when he saw something exciting. There was a large, brand-new merry-go-round—right in the middle of the Main Street!

"Mom!" he whispered, tugging at her coat. "Mom! Can I go on that?" Mom agreed, and Danny raced over to the merry-go-round. It had blue and yellow stripes, with white, prancing horses. Danny bought a ticket and climbed onto one of the horses. It had a yellow saddle and one leg held up in the air.

"You look like a fast horse," said Danny, patting its mane. The music began and the horses started to move.

"Giddy up!" shouted Danny. "Faster!" The merry-go-round whirled so fast that soon the town and the stores were a blur.

When the ride slowed down, the town had completely disappeared! Instead, Danny found himself in the middle of a magical fairground wonderland. There were amazing rides all around. He could hardly wait to try them out. As he ran through the fairground he saw faces that he knew. The wolf from Red Riding Hood was testing his strength. Little Bo Beep was taking a break from searching for her sheep, and Georgie Porgie was munching on some pie.

Danny whizzed down the crazy slide. He rode on dancing bees and whirled around on the dish that ran away with the spoon. There was a pirate treasure roller coaster and a boat ride around the fairground. He flew down the monkey slides and flew up and around on the Itsy Bitsy Spider ride. It was the best fun Danny had ever had!

After Danny had been on every ride twice, he followed one of the Three Little Pigs to a market. There were stalls selling pots of delicious honey, gingerbread men, and iced cupcakes, as well as elegant hats and the biggest, brightest balloons Danny had ever seen. He bought armfuls of crusty bread, candies, pies, and cookies, and a basket of ripe, delicious fruit and vegetables. When he couldn't carry any more, he knew that it was time to go home.

Danny climbed back onto the prancing white horse, holding on tightly to his parcels. The horses started to move. Faster! Faster! The merry-go-round turned the fairground into a blur, and then slowed down. Danny was back in the high street again. He slipped off the horse and waved at Mom, who was coming out of the grocer's.

"Goodness me, where did you get all that food?" she exclaimed. "I've only been in the grocer's for two minutes!"

Danny looked back at the merry-go-round and grinned.
"I'll tell you all about it, Mom," he said. "As long as you
promise to bring me back here tomorrow!"

1

Little Boy Blue

Little Boy Blue,
Come blow your horn.
The sheep's in the meadow,
The cow's in the corn.
Where is the boy who looks after the sheep?
He's under a haycock, fast asleep.
Will you wake him?
No, not I, for if I do, he's sure to cry.

B-I-N-G-O!

There was a farmer had a dog,
And Bingo was his name-o.
B-I-N-G-O
B-I-N-G-O
B-I-N-G-O
And Bingo was his name-o.

Robin and Richard

Robin and Richard were two pretty men,
They lay in bed till the clock struck ten;
Then up starts Robin, and looks at the sky,
"Oh! Oh! Brother Richard, the sun's very high,
You go before with bottle and bag,
And I'll follow after on little Jack Nag."

Gray Goose and Gander

Gray goose and gander,
Waft your wings together,
And carry the good king's daughter
Over the one-strand river.

Old Mother Goose

Old Mother Goose, when
She wanted to wander,
Would ride through the air
On a very fine gander.

Cock-a-Doodle-Doo!

Cock-a-doodle-doo!
My dame has lost her shoe!
My master's lost his fiddling stick,
And doesn't know what to do.

183

Catch of the Day

Simon had been fishing all day. "All I've got in my net is clams!" he shouted. "I'm not leaving without a fish!"

The sea creatures gathered underwater. "Let's show him what we can do," said a little crab. Fish leaped out of the water and jellyfish danced on the waves. Dolphins hopped across the surface on their tail fins, balancing crabs on their noses.

"Help!" Simon yelled as an octopus tried to climb into his boat. "Please don't eat me!" Then he stared at the beautiful sea creatures that were dancing and splashing around his boat. "Oh I see," he exclaimed. "You don't want to me to catch you because you don't want to be eaten either!"

Simon smiled and emptied his fishing net of clams. "I will never try to catch you again," he promised. "Keep dancing in the sea, where you belong!"

Big Bug Adventure

Omar loved bugs. One sunny day, he was watching the beetles in the garden and picking them up whenever they fell onto their backs. Soon the hot sun made him yawn and he fell asleep.

When he awoke, he was amazed to see that the blade of grass beside him was as big as a lamppost! "Help!" Omar squeaked as a crowd of giant beetles, spiders, and ants scurried toward him.

"Don't be scared!" they called. "We want to make friends, because you're always so kind to us!"

Being insect-sized was great! Omar crawled into the woodpile where the woodlice lived. He climbed spiders' webs and explored the tunnels that the ants dug. He played with the bugs all afternoon, and when the sun set, a dragonfly carried him up to his room. In the morning, he was back to his usual size. But he would never forget his new bug friends!

Bathtime for Bertie

Mommy Elephant swayed her trunk as she walked through the long grass toward the trees lining the river.

"Bertie!" she called loudly. "It's bathtime. We need to go to the river before the light fades."

Bertie the baby elephant flapped his ears in a panic, and ran to hide behind the large baobab tree.

"I'm not here!" called Bertie.

"I can see your little swishy tail!" laughed Mommy.

Bertie loved living on the vast African plain. He loved running through the long grass. And best of all he loved rolling in the dusty mud with Mommy.

But he did not like bathtime at all!

"I'm afraid of the river," sobbed Bertie. "The water moves so quickly. I'm frightened it will sweep me away!"

"Don't worry, I'll stay by your side the whole time, I promise," Mommy said, gently.

Holding on to Mommy's tail, Bertie slowly waded into the shallow water by the riverbank.

"If you put your feet like this," explained Mommy Elephant, showing Bertie how to stand in the water, "you won't fall over."

Bertie moved his feet. The water swirled past, but he didn't fall.

Mommy gently sprayed some water over Bertie's head.

Bertie giggled loudly. The cool water felt lovely as it trickled down his back.

"Maybe bathtime isn't so bad after all!" laughed Bertie. "I can't wait for my bath tomorrow!"

Super Robot

Tommy and Timmy were brothers. They both liked football, they both disliked broccoli, and they both loved robots. But they rooted for different football teams. They tried to sneak broccoli onto each other's plates at dinner time. And they each wanted to win their town's Build A Robot competition.

Tommy and Timmy worked hard to make their robots and dreamed of beating each other. On the day of the competition, the organizer asked them what their robots did. "Mine's super strong," said Timmy. "It can lift anything!"

"Mine's super fast," said Tommy, pushing Timmy to one side. "It's quicker than a jet!"

Just then the organizer got a phone call. "Bad news," she said. "The judge's car has broken down miles away. I'll have to cancel the competition!"

Timmy and Tommy looked at each other. If they put their robots together, they could rescue the judge and save the competition. But could they forget their differences?

The brothers hammered, welded and twiddled until they had built one giant super robot. Then they opened the control panel and tapped in their instructions. BEEP BEEP! The robot nodded and then ZOOM! It was gone!

The crowd held their breath as it sped out of sight. Could it rescue the judge? Then the robot reappeared, carrying the judge's car above its head. It put the car down and the judge stepped out.

"Who made this amazing robot?" he asked, smiling.

Tommy and Timmy stepped forward, arm in arm.

"What great teamwork," said the judge. "You are the joint winners of the competition!"

Tommy and Timmy grinned at each other. Winning was wonderful, but the best part was working as a team!

Hot Cross Buns

Hot cross buns!
Hot cross buns!
One-a-penny, two-a-penny,
Hot cross buns!
If you have no daughters,
Give them to your sons,
One-a-penny, two-a-penny,
Hot cross buns!

Wash Hands

Wash, hands, wash,
Daddy's gone to plow;
If you want your hands wash'd,
Have them wash'd now.

Willie Wastle

I, Willie Wastle,
Stand on my castle,
An' a' the dogs o' your toon,
Will no' drive Willie Wastle down.

Richard Dick

Richard Dick upon a stick,
Sampson on a sow,
We'll ride away to Colley fair
To buy a horse to plow.

Parliament Soldiers

High diddle ding, did you hear the bells ring?
The parliament soldiers are gone to the king.
Some they did laugh, and some they did cry,
To see the parliament soldiers go by.

Oats and Beans

Oats and beans and barley grow,
Oats and beans and barley grow,
Do you or I or anyone know,
How oats and beans and barley grow?

First the farmer sows his seeds,
Then he stands and takes his ease,
Stamps his feet and claps his hands,
Turns around to view the land.

How the Tiger Got His Stripes

A very long time ago, when the tiger had no stripes upon his back and the rabbit still had a long tail, there was a tiger who owned a farm. As his farm was very overgrown with undergrowth, the tiger decided to look for a worker to clear the ground for him so he could plant his crops.

The tiger called all the animals together. "I need a good workman to clear the undergrowth. I will give an ox in payment to whoever does the work," he said.

A monkey, a goat, and an armadillo applied for the job, but when the tiger tried them out, they didn't do the work to his satisfaction, and he dismissed them all without payment.

Finally a little rabbit applied for the position. The tiger laughed at him, "You are too small to do the work!"

But as there were no other applicants for the job, the tiger decided to give the rabbit a try.

The rabbit worked hard and after a week he had cleared a large area of the ground. For the next few days the rabbit continued to work hard until he had cleared all the ground. The tiger was very pleased. He gave the rabbit the ox as promised.

The rabbit took the ox and went off to find a spot to kill it and have his lunch. Just as he was about to eat the ox, the tiger appeared from the bushes nearby.

"O, rabbit, I'm so very hungry!" cried the tiger. "Look, you can see my ribs. As you are such a good friend of mine, won't you be so kind as to give me a piece of your ox to eat?"

The rabbit gave the tiger a piece of the ox. The tiger devoured it immediately.

"Is that all you are going to give me to eat?" asked the sly tiger.

The tiger looked so big and savage that the rabbit didn't dare to refuse him any more of the ox. Soon the tiger had devoured the entire ox, leaving only a tiny morsel for the poor rabbit.

The rabbit was furious with the tiger. A few days later he went to a place near the tiger's farm and began cutting big sticks of wood.

The tiger saw the rabbit and wondered what he was doing.

"Oh, haven't you heard?" said the rabbit. "The order has gone forth that every beast should build a barrier around themselves, to protect them from hunters."

The tiger was alarmed. "Oh, no! Rabbit, what shall I do?" he cried. "I don't know how to build a barrier. As you are my dear friend, won't you help me first before you build your own barrier?"

The rabbit sighed and agreed to help him. He built a strong barrier around the tiger using strong sticks, and fastened more sticks over the top until the tiger was completely shut in. Then he left.

The tiger waited and waited for something to happen. Nothing did and he grew very hungry and thirsty.

Then he heard some animals passing by. It was the monkey, goat, and armadillo.

"Oh, dear friends," roared the tiger. "Has the danger passed? Can you help me out of here?"

The animals were still angry at the tiger about the work on his farm. "Yes, the danger has passed," they lied. "Let the one who got you in there help you out." And they walked away.

It was hot inside the enclosed barrier and the tiger could feel the sun burning stripes in his fur through the gaps between the sticks. Desperately, he threw himself with all his might at the bars, until finally, he broke through.

And that is how the tiger got his stripes.

Brown Owl

The brown owl sits in the ivy-bush,
And she looketh wondrous wise,
With a horny beak beneath her cowl,
And a pair of large round eyes.

Butterfly, Butterfly

"Butterfly, butterfly,
Where do you go?"
"Where the sun shines,
And where the buds grow."

Ladybird, Ladybird

Ladybird, ladybird, fly away home;
Your house is on fire, your children all gone,
All except one, and that's little Ann,
And she hid under the baking pan.

Goosey, Goosey, Gander

Goosey, goosey, gander,
Whither do you wander?
Upstairs and downstairs
And in my lady's chamber.
There I met an old man
Who would not say his prayers,
So I took him by the left leg,
And threw him down the stairs.

Dandy

I had a dog and his name was Dandy,
His tail was long and his legs were bandy,
His eyes were brown and his coat was sandy,
The best in the world was my dog Dandy.

I Had a Little Puppy

I had a little puppy,
His name was Tiny Tim.
I put him in the bathtub,
To see if he could swim.
He drank all the water,
He ate a bar of soap—
The next thing I know
He had a bubble in his throat!

X Marks the Spot

Jim's best friend Aaron was a lot of fun, but there was just one problem. He was very, very forgetful.

One day they were exploring in Aaron's garden when they found a treasure map.

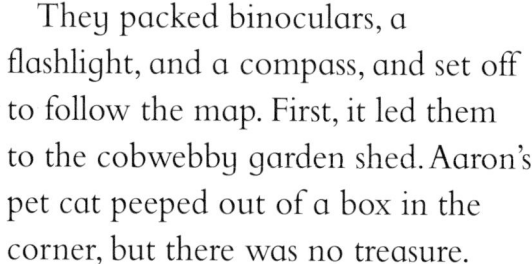

"X marks the spot!" Jim exclaimed. "Let's follow the map and find the treasure."

They packed binoculars, a flashlight, and a compass, and set off to follow the map. First, it led them to the cobwebby garden shed. Aaron's pet cat peeped out of a box in the corner, but there was no treasure.

"Where is it?" asked Aaron.

"We need to find the X," said Jim. "X marks the spot."

"Oh, yes, I forgot," said Aaron.

Next, the map pointed Jim, Aaron, and the cat to the bird bath on the lawn. A magpie was splashing around in it, but there was no treasure.

"Where is it?" asked Aaron.

"X marks the spot, remember?" said Jim.

"Oh yes, I forgot," said Aaron. "Silly me!"

Jim, Aaron, the cat, and the magpie followed the map until they reached the biggest tree in the garden.

"Look!" exclaimed Aaron. "Someone's taped a big X on the trunk! I wonder why?"

"Because X marks the spot where the treasure is hidden," Jim reminded him.

Aaron gasped. "I forgot! The map shows where I hid the candies my sister gave me last Christmas. I made it to help me remember—and then I lost the map!"

Aaron took the candies out of a hole in the tree and shared them out. They were wrapped in shiny golden paper, and Jim grinned.

"This is really the best treasure I can imagine!" he said.

Tumbling

In jumping and tumbling we spend the whole day,
Till night by arriving has finished our play
What then? One and all, there's no more to be said,
As we tumbled all day, so we tumble to bed.

Lie a-Bed

Lie a-bed,
Sleepy head,
Shut up eyes, bo-peep;
Till day-break
Never wake:
Baby, sleep.

There Was a Crooked Man

There was a crooked man, and he went a crooked mile,
He found a crooked sixpence against a crooked stile;
He bought a crooked cat, which caught a crooked mouse,
And they all lived together in a little crooked house.

Three Wise Men of Gotham

Three wise men of Gotham
Went to sea in a bowl:
And if the bowl had been stronger
My song would have been longer.

I Hear Thunder

I hear thunder, I hear thunder,
Hark! don't you? Hark! don't you?
Pitter, patter raindrops, pitter, patter raindrops,
I'm wet through, I'm wet through.

Pop Goes the Weasel

Half a pound of tuppenny rice,
Half a pound of treacle
That's the way the money goes,
Pop! goes the weasel.

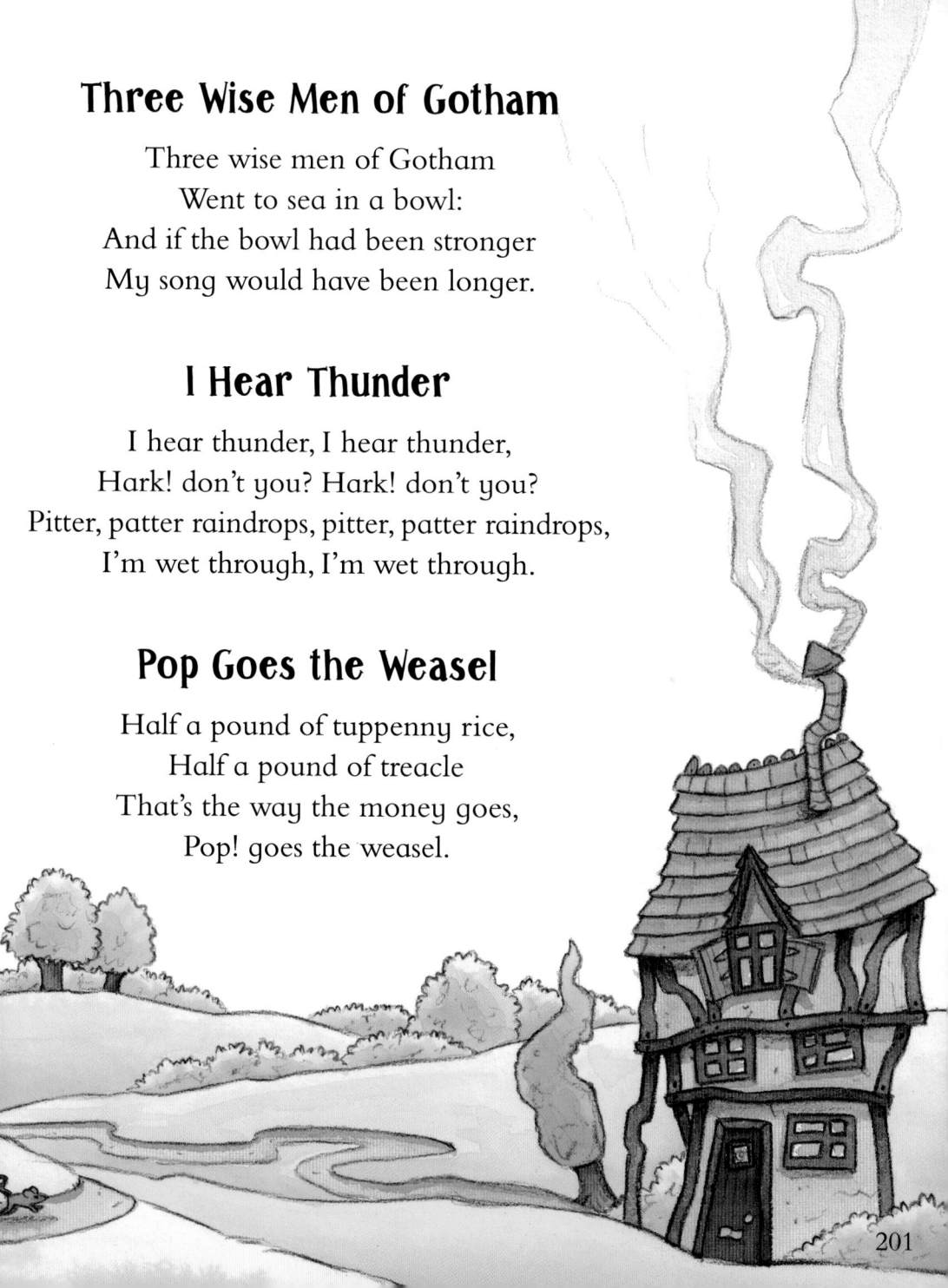

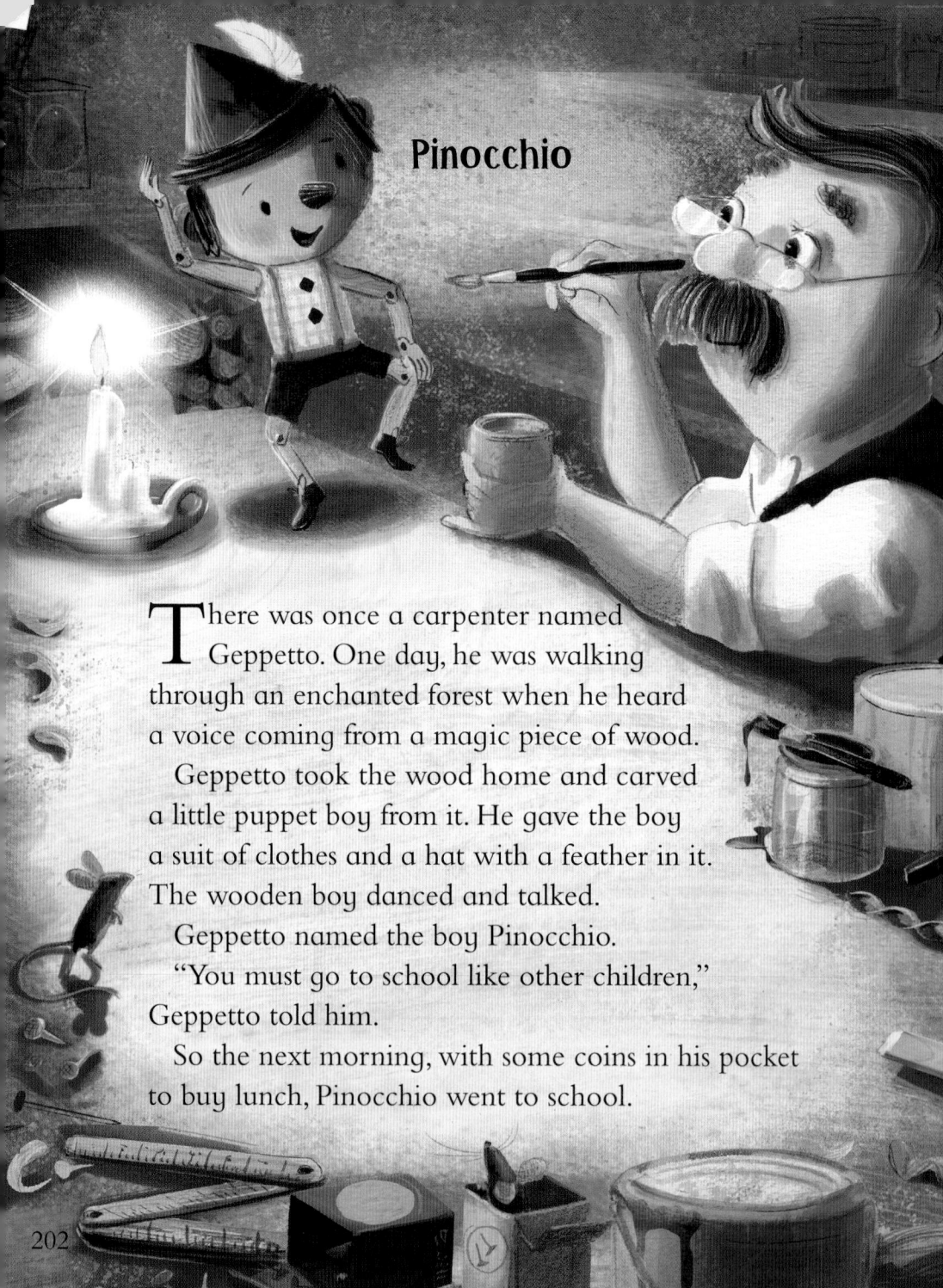

Pinocchio

There was once a carpenter named Geppetto. One day, he was walking through an enchanted forest when he heard a voice coming from a magic piece of wood.

Geppetto took the wood home and carved a little puppet boy from it. He gave the boy a suit of clothes and a hat with a feather in it. The wooden boy danced and talked.

Geppetto named the boy Pinocchio.

"You must go to school like other children," Geppetto told him.

So the next morning, with some coins in his pocket to buy lunch, Pinocchio went to school.

Along the way, a cricket hopped up onto his shoulder.

"You look like you could use a friend," he told Pinocchio. "I will help you learn right from wrong."

Farther down the road, Pinocchio met a fox and a cat. They had heard his money jangling in his pocket.

"Come and play with us!" said the fox slyly.

"Pinocchio, you promised your father you would go to school," the cricket whispered.

But Pinocchio, not knowing any better, followed the cat and the fox into a dark forest.

"Plant your money here, and it will grow into a money tree," they told Pinocchio. "Just come back tomorrow, and you'll see."

The next morning, instead of going to school, Pinocchio went to find his money tree. But when he reached the spot where he'd buried his coins, there was no money tree, and his coins had gone.

"They played a trick on you," sighed his friend, the cricket. "They just wanted to get your money."

Pinocchio felt silly, but he pretended he didn't care, and stomped off into the forest. The little cricket begged him to go back to Geppetto, but Pinocchio wouldn't listen. Just as it was getting dark, they came to a tiny cottage. Pinocchio knocked on the door loudly and a pretty fairy answered.

"We're lost," explained Pinocchio. "Please can you help us?"

The fairy invited them in and gave them some food.

"Why are you so far from home?" she asked kindly.

Pinocchio didn't want to tell her that he had disobeyed his father.

"I was chased by a giant!" he lied.

Suddenly, Pinocchio's nose grew a little.

"And I ran into the forest to escape!" he continued.

And Pinocchio's nose grew again!

"I have put a spell on you!" said the fairy. "Every time you tell a lie, your wooden nose will grow."

Pinocchio began to cry. "I won't tell any more lies," he promised.

The fairy waved her wand and Pinocchio's nose returned to normal.

"From now on I will do just as Father tells me," he said. But when he returned home, Geppetto wasn't there. He was out searching for Pinocchio!

"We must find Father and bring him home," he sobbed, feeling bad.

They began their search by the river. But when they got there, Pinocchio fell into the water. The cricket jumped in to help him, but an enormous fish swallowed them both.

There in the fish's tummy, they found Geppetto! He had been swallowed by the fish too.

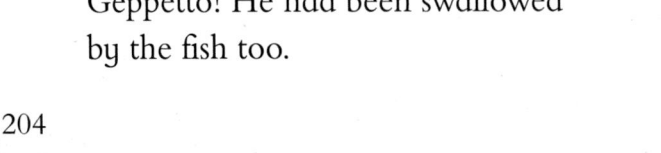

Pinocchio hugged his father tightly. "I won't leave you again!" he said.

Then Pinocchio took the feather from his hat and tickled the fish.

"A ... a ... a ... choo!" The fish gave a mighty sneeze and Geppetto, Pinocchio, and the cricket flew out of the fish's mouth, and landed on the riverbank.

That night, as Pinocchio slept in his own little bed, the kind fairy flew in through his window.

"You're a good, brave boy," she said, and she kissed him on the forehead.

When Pinocchio awoke the next morning, he found that he was no longer made from wood. He was a real boy! From then on he was always a good son to Geppetto, and the best of friends with the cricket, who didn't need to tell him right from wrong ever again.

Jack, Jack, the Bread's a-Burning

Jack, Jack, the bread's a-burning,
All to a cinder;
If you don't come and fetch it out
We'll throw it through the window.

Five Little Peas

Five little peas in a pea pod pressed,
One grew, two grew, and so did all the rest.
They grew, and they grew, and they did not stop,
Until one day the pod went ... POP!

Higgledy Piggledy

Higgledy piggledy,
Here we lie,
Picked and plucked,
And put in a pie!

Pease Pudding Hot

Pease pudding hot, pease pudding cold,
Pease pudding in the pot, nine days old.
Some like it hot, some like it cold,
Some like it in the pot, nine days old!

Here's the Lady's Knives and Forks

Here's the lady's knives and forks.
Here's the lady's table.
Here's the lady's looking glass.
And here's the baby's cradle.
Rock! Rock! Rock! Rock!

Bread and Milk for Breakfast

Bread and milk for breakfast,
And woolen frocks to wear,
And a crumb for robin redbreast
On the cold days of the year.

Island Adventure

Captain Nat and her friends were sailing in their boat, looking for adventures. Nat scanned the sea with her telescope. "Land ho!" she shouted. "There's an island ahead!"

They dropped the anchor and rowed to shore in a little dinghy. Airplanes roared overhead and a steam train chugged across the island. There were shiny sports cars racing around a track, and speedboats pulling waterskiers through the waves.

"What an amazing island!" said First Mate Peggy. "Time to explore. Let's go!"

The crew jumped into the little blue train and the whistle blew. Chugga-chugga, chugga-chugga. They were off on a tour of the island. It was filled with exciting vehicles of every shape and size.

There were helicopters, backhoes, tractors, and motorcycless. But best of all, they were all just the right size for children, and a big sign said "No Grown-ups Allowed."

"Let's have a competition," said Chief Cook Corin. "The first one to have a ride in all the vehicles is the winner!"

Captain Nat and her cabin boys Jake and Fraser jumped into an airplane. First Mate Peggy leaped onto a motorbike and Chief Cook Corin took the train. Vroom vroom! Zoom zoom! Soon the crew was whizzing all over the island, trying the fastest, loudest vehicles they could find. It was a close race! They all arrived back on the beach at the same time, and raced over the sand to the dinghy. But the winner was Captain Nat.

"Three cheers for the captain!" shouted First Mate Peggy. "But what's her prize?"

"I'm allowed to steer the ship home," said Captain Nat with a grin. "Anchors aweigh!"

When the Moon Came Along

Avery long time ago, there was only the sun, and no moon. The sun shone all the time, day and night. People worked until they were too tired to work any more.

Because there was no day and night, people had no idea when to sleep. So the sun decided to set in the evening and rise in the morning. When it got dark, people would stop working and rest.

At first people were afraid of the dark. They couldn't see, and they often fell over or broke things.

People were happier now there was night and day, but they still wanted to see when it went dark.

And so the moon came along, with a peaceful moonlight glow. People could now see at night. They could sleep peacefully and wake up rested to work the next day in the sunlight.

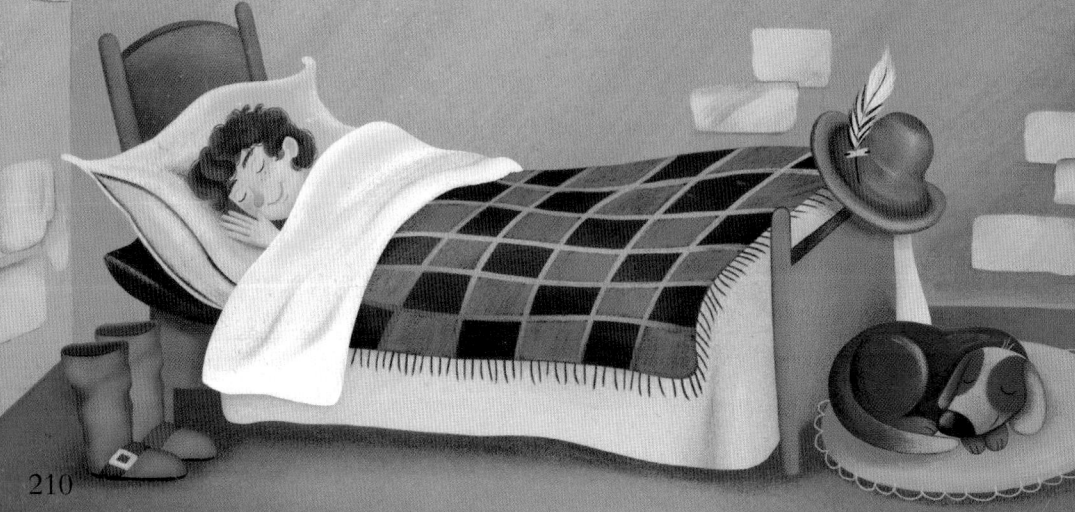

A Poor Man's Dream

A long time ago, there lived a Brahmin—a Hindu priest. He was very poor and sometimes he went without food for many days.

One day, the Brahmin was given a pot full of flour to make bread with. He was very happy and placed the pot near his bed. Soon, he fell fast asleep and started to dream.

He dreamed that a famine came to the land and that he sold his flour for a huge pile of silver coins. With the coins he bought some cows. The Brahmin made butter from the cows' milk to sell in the market. He soon became very rich, built himself a large house and married a beautiful girl. They had many sons and daughters.

The Brahmin's legs kicked out in his sleep, knocking the pot over. He woke with a start. There was no big house, no silver coins, or wife and children. All he had was a broken pot and flour scattered over his floor.

The Nose that Knows

Milo loves his owner.
She's a girl named Molly Brown.
But Milo's nose loves food the most ...
it leads him all round town.

For Milo's nose is a nose that knows—
it knows when food is near.
When it smells a smell, the nose soon shows
poor Milo where to steer!

Molly's heading out with Mom.
Milo wants to come too. BARK! BARK!
But the nose has sniffed a SANDWICH
moving quickly through the park.

Where the nose goes, Milo goes ... SPLASH!
So now he's paddling through a pond!
Then his nose smells a smell of which
he's really rather fond ...!

213

... Crunchy, munchy APPLES.

They're in a massive rocket—
he'll just grab one and then he'll go.
He sneaks in, but the doors close.

FOUR

THREE

TWO

ONE ...

WHOOSH, ZOOM!
Milo's flying to the moon!

Out he climbs, and finds the moon is
made of PEANUT BUTTER!

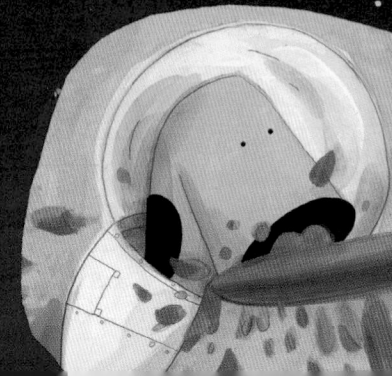

But then his nose smells something oh so nice!
It's miles away, but it smells just like paradise!
His nose, it knows what's cooking—his favorite thing to eat ...
Cooking on a barbecue, it's yummy, sizzling MEAT!

"Hey! You're back!" cries Molly. "Wherever did you go?"
Milo wags his tail, but she will never know!
Molly's just glad he's home and gives him ONE HUGE TREAT!
Milo's glad to be back too, and glad—at last—to eat.

So Milo, he might wander. Yes Milo, he might roam.
But Milo's nose is a nose that knows and will always lead him to ...

MOLLY, FOOD, and HOME!

Little Jack Horner

Little Jack Horner sat in the corner,
Eating his Christmas pie;
He put in his thumb, and pulled out a plum,
And said, "What a good boy am I!"

Betty Botter Bought Some Butter

Betty Botter bought some butter,
But she said, "The butter's bitter.
If I put it in my batter,
It will make my batter bitter.
But a bit of better butter
Will make my batter better."
So she bought some better butter.
Better than the bitter butter,
And she put it in her batter.
And her batter was not bitter.
So 'twas better Betty Botter
Bought a bit of better butter.

Georgie Porgie

Georgie Porgie, pudding and pie,
Kissed the girls, and made them cry.
When the boys came out to play,
Georgie Porgie ran away.

Yankee Doodle

Yankee Doodle went to town,
Riding on a pony;
He stuck a feather in his cap
And called it macaroni.

The Golden Goose

There was once a poor boy named Billy, who lived with his family at the edge of a forest. One day when he was cutting wood, an old man approached him.

"Could I please share some of your food?" the man asked.

"Of course," said Billy, although he barely had enough food for himself.

"Thank you," said the old man. "You shall be rewarded. Cut down that tree over there and see what's inside it."

So he did. Hidden inside the tree trunk was a goose with golden feathers! Puzzled, Billy looked around for the old man, but he had mysteriously vanished.

It was getting too dark to walk home, so Billy picked up the goose and took it with him to an inn.

The innkeeper's three daughters were fascinated by the goose's golden feathers. But when the eldest girl tried to take one, she stuck fast to the goose. As her sisters tried to pull her away, they all got stuck to each other.

The next morning, Billy set off down the street with the golden goose, dragging the girls behind him.

When other people saw the strange scene, they tried to pull the girls free, only to become stuck too!

Meanwhile, the king had a daughter who never laughed. The king was so desperate to cheer her up that he had promised her hand in marriage to anyone who could make her happy.

When the princess looked out of her palace window that day, she saw Billy walking along the street carrying a golden goose with a line of people staggering behind. The princess laughed and laughed.

The king was delighted. "You made the princess laugh!" he told Billy. "That means you may marry her!"

"Me?" Billy cried, just as the goose jumped from his arms. All the people toppled backward, unstuck, and the princess laughed again.

So Billy and the princess soon married, and they lived long, happy lives full of laughter.

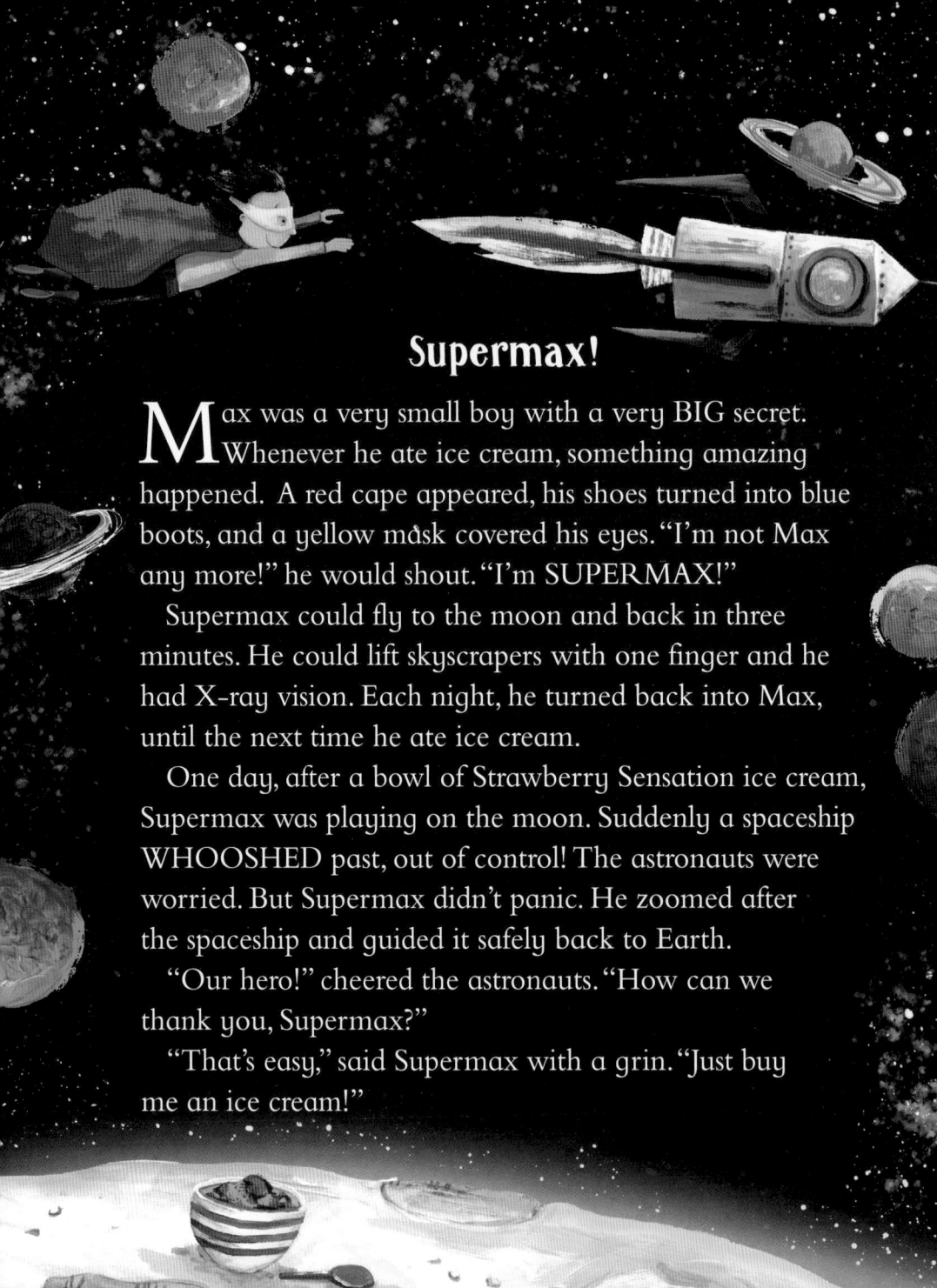

Supermax!

Max was a very small boy with a very BIG secret. Whenever he ate ice cream, something amazing happened. A red cape appeared, his shoes turned into blue boots, and a yellow mask covered his eyes. "I'm not Max any more!" he would shout. "I'm SUPERMAX!"

Supermax could fly to the moon and back in three minutes. He could lift skyscrapers with one finger and he had X-ray vision. Each night, he turned back into Max, until the next time he ate ice cream.

One day, after a bowl of Strawberry Sensation ice cream, Supermax was playing on the moon. Suddenly a spaceship WHOOSHED past, out of control! The astronauts were worried. But Supermax didn't panic. He zoomed after the spaceship and guided it safely back to Earth.

"Our hero!" cheered the astronauts. "How can we thank you, Supermax?"

"That's easy," said Supermax with a grin. "Just buy me an ice cream!"

Super Shoes

Luke's dad invented all sorts of peculiar things, but his latest invention was the strangest yet.

"Special shoes!" he said, as Luke put them on. "I want you to try them out for a day and tell me what you think."

"What do they do?" asked Luke.

"You'll see," said his dad.

At first, Luke's friends laughed.

"You look silly!" they said. "Those shoes aren't cool!"

But they soon changed their minds when they saw what the shoes could do. During gym class, the springs in the heels made Luke leap the highest. In the playground, roller-skate wheels popped out of the soles. At recess, a shower of candy burst from the toes!
At the end of the day, all Luke's friends wanted a pair.

"Sorry Luke," his dad chuckled. "My inventions are all one-offs. I have just invented a jacket with wings attached. Will you wear it to school tomorrow?"

"Definitely!" said Luke.

The Farmer and the Badger

Long, long ago, there lived an old farmer and his wife. Their only neighbor was a bad badger. Every night the badger would pull up the farmer's vegetables and cause damage on his farm. The old farmer could not stand it any more, so one night he laid a trap and caught the wicked animal.

The next day, he told his wife to keep an eye on the badger, while he went to work.

"When I get back, we will make him into soup," he said.

The clever badger did not want to be made into soup, so he decided to trick the old woman into releasing him.

"You look very tired," said the badger in a sweet, sad voice. "Why don't you untie me and I can help you with the chores."

The old woman had a kind heart, so she untied the cunning beast, and sat down for a rest.

As soon as he was free, the badger bared his teeth and scared her so much she ran away and didn't come back. Then, disguised as the old woman, the badger waited for the farmer to return.

When the farmer came home, the badger threw off his disguise and told the farmer what he had done before running away.

The poor farmer was distraught. A kind rabbit who lived over the valley heard his loud wailing and came to see what was wrong. When he heard the farmer's sad tale, he decided to help him get his revenge on the wicked badger.

The next day, the rabbit went to visit the badger.

"It's such a beautiful day, come fishing with me," he said.

The badger thought this sounded fun, so he agreed.

The rabbit had made two boats, one out of wood and one out of clay. He gave the clay boat to the badger.

"Let's race to the middle of the lake," laughed the rabbit.

As the badger rowed across the lake, his boat, being made of clay, began to soften and fall to pieces, and he tumbled into the water. And that was the end of the wicked badger!

Just the Way You Are!

One day there was a knock on Frank the rabbit's mossy front door. It was his best friend, James.

"It's my birthday and I'm having a party," said James. "I want to invite all my rabbit friends, and you're top of the list!"

Frank the rabbit loved dancing. He danced in the street. He danced when he went shopping. He even danced in his sleep. But wherever he was dancing, it ended the same way. He always got overexcited, thumped his big feet on the ground, thumpity-thumpity-thumpity-thump, and made everything come crashing down around him. Disaster! People always got annoyed with Frank, even though he never meant to be naughty.

"James, you know what happens if I go to parties," Frank said, groaning. "I always end up breaking things with my big feet and upsetting everyone."

"You could never upset me," said James, putting his arm around Frank. "You're my best friend. Please come."

Frank looked at his smiling friend and had to say yes. So later that day, he arrived at the party feeling very nervous indeed.

"Definitely no dancing," he told his feet. "No tapping. And definitely no thumpity-thumpity-thumpity-thumping!"

At first, everything went well. Frank played hide-and-seek and
ate three cupcakes. But then someone turned the music on, and
the first song was Frank's favorite. First, his big toe on one foot
started tapping. Then all his toes ... then both feet. And then—
oh dear—Frank was leaping and hopping and bopping to the
music. He spun and slid and whirled and twirled. He flung his
arms and kicked up his legs. He forgot all about being careful.
CRASH! The plates of party food flew through the air. He
bounced into the air, spinning, and his ears got tangled up
in the party decorations. They all came tumbling down around
the other guests.

The song ended, and Frank looked around at the mess. His heart sank.

"I've done it again," he said with a groan. "I'm so so sorry, James," he said.

James looked surprised. "What are you sorry for?" he asked.

"I've spoiled your party with my dancing," said Frank, and his ears drooped. But James gave him a big hug.

"You silly billy!" he said with a laugh. "You haven't spoiled my party! Everyone loved your dancing. Look!"

He pointed at the other guests. No one was looking cross or tidying up the mess. In fact, they were making it worse! They were tapping, thumping and jiving to the music. Everyone was copying Frank's dance moves, and they all looked very happy.

A big smile spread across Frank's face.

"I thought I had to change to fit in with everyone else," he said.

"I don't want you to change a single thing," said James.
"Dancing makes you happy, so it makes me happy too.
You're my best friend—and I like you just the way you are!"

Jack Sprat

Jack Sprat could eat no fat,
His wife could eat no lean,
And so between the two of them
They licked the platter clean.

Poor Old Robinson Crusoe!

Poor old Robinson Crusoe!
Poor old Robinson Crusoe!
They made him a coat of an old nanny goat,
I wonder how they could do so!
With a ring a ting tang,
And a ring a ting tang,
Poor old Robinson Crusoe!

Rub-a-Dub Dub

Rub-a-dub dub, three men in a tub,
And who do you think they be?
The butcher, the baker, the candle-stick maker,
Turn them out knaves all three.

Solomon Grundy

Solomon Grundy
Born on Monday,
Christened on Tuesday,
Married on Wednesday,
Sick on Thursday,
Worse on Friday
Died on Saturday,
Buried on Sunday,
That was the end
Of Solomon Grundy.

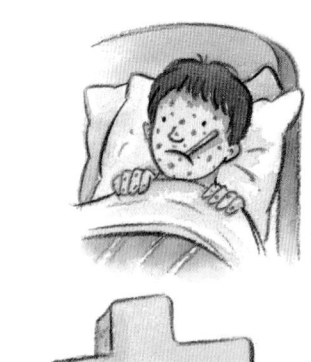

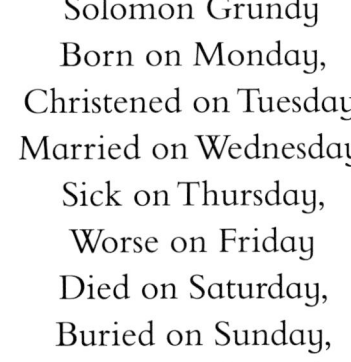

Me, Myself, and I

Me, myself, and I—
We went to the kitchen and ate a pie.
Then my mother she came in
And chased us out with a rolling pin.

Swan Swam Over the Sea

Swan swam over the sea—
Swim, swan, swim,
Swan swam back again,
Well swum swan.

The Two Brothers

Once upon a time there were two brothers who lived at the bottom of a mountain. One was rich, but cruel and selfish; the other was poor, but kind and honest. The poor brother had many children, and the day came when there was not enough food in the house to feed them all. He went to his rich brother to ask him for a loaf of bread, but the wicked man threw him out and called him a beggar.

The poor man couldn't face returning home empty-handed. It was a cold evening and he remembered having heard a legend that the top of the mountain in front of him was made of crystal and had a fire forever burning on it.

"I will try and find this eternal fire, and warm myself up," he said. "Then I will have the strength to find some food for my family."

The man climbed higher and higher up the mountain until he reached the top. There, sitting around a fire, were twelve strange beings.

"Good people," whispered the man, "please let me warm myself at your fire."

"Of course," replied one of the twelve. "Come and sit with us."

When the man drew near, an old man appeared in the flames.

"Return home with as many embers as you need," said the strange vision.

The twelve strangers filled a sack with embers. Humbly thanking them, the man set off. To his astonishment, when he arrived home, he found the sack to be full of gold pieces. The poor man was now rich and could provide for his family. He was overjoyed at the kindness of the strangers on the mountain.

When his greedy, rich brother heard of his good fortune, he decided to go up the mountain to get his own gold.

When he arrived, he told the twelve strangers that he was poor and cold. But instead of giving him a sack of gold, the strangers turned on him.

"You have lied to us. You shall be punished!" they cried. They took him to the old man in the fire and the rich brother disappeared into the flames.

Months went by and the rich man didn't return home. No one knew what had happened to him. His brother had his suspicions, but wisely kept them to himself.

I Plant a Little Seed

I plant a little seed in the cold, cold ground,
Out comes the yellow sun, big and round,
Down come the raindrops, soft and slow,
Up comes the flower, grow, grow, grow.

One Man Went to Mow

One man went to mow,
Went to mow a meadow,
One man and his dog,
Went to mow a meadow.
Two men went to mow,
Went to mow a meadow,
Two men, one man, and his dog,
Went to mow a meadow.

*You can keep adding verses
as far as you can count.*

A Swarm of Bees in May

A swarm of bees in May is worth a load of hay;
A swarm of bees in June is worth a silver spoon;
A swarm of bees in July is not worth a fly.

Four Seeds in a Row

Four seeds in a row,
Four seeds in a row.
One for the mouse,
One for the crow,
One to rot and one to grow.

Grinding Corn

Early in the misty morn,
The miller's up to grind some corn.
Wheels turn, sacks will fill,
As he grinds corn in his mill.

Rikki-Tikki-Tavi

Rikki-Tikki-Tavi was a small furry mongoose. He lived a happy life with his parents in the jungle. Then one day, a great summer flood washed him from his burrow. He was swept into a roadside ditch.

When he revived, Rikki-Tikki-Tavi was lying in the middle of a path in front of a house.

"Look, Mom! A mongoose," cried a young boy.

"The poor little thing is exhausted," said the boy's mother. "Let's take him in to dry."

The little boy was named Teddy and he lived in the bungalow with his parents. The family were so kind that Rikki-Tikki-Tavi decided to stay.

One day when Rikki-Tikki-Tavi was exploring the yard, he heard somebody crying. It was Darzee, the tailorbird and his wife.

"What's the matter?" asked Rikki-Tikki-Tavi.

"Nag, the black cobra, has eaten one of our babies," sobbed Darzee, as a hideous snake slithered into sight.

"I'm Nag," hissed the snake. "Be very afraid."

Rikki-Tikki-Tavi did feel afraid, but he knew it was every brave mongoose's duty to fight deadly snakes. He held his little tail high and puffed out his cheeks. He looked terrifying and Nag began to shake.

"Watch out behind you!" cried Darzee.

Nagaina, Nag's wicked wife, had crept up behind Rikki-Tikki-Tavi. He leaped into the air and just missed being struck by her. The two snakes slithered off into the tall grass.

"I'm going to need all my strength to fight Nag and his wife," said Rikki-Tikki-Tavi. "I must protect my new family and friends."

That night, when Teddy was safely asleep in bed, Rikki-Tikki-Tavi crept out into the yard. He could hear Nag and Nagaina whispering in a dark corner.

"We'll bite the big man first," hissed Nag. "Once the humans are gone, that mongoose will have to go."

"Yes," agreed his wife. "We'll need the space in the yard as soon as our eggs in the melon bed hatch."

Rikki-Tikki-Tavi shook with rage at hearing this, but he hid as the giant cobra slithered into the bathroom, ready to bite Teddy's father in the morning.

As soon as Nag fell asleep, Rikki-Tikki-Tavi pounced. He sank his fangs into the cobra's head and held on as the huge snake thrashed around. Rikki-Tikki-Tavi was sure he was going to be beaten to death. Then, suddenly, a gun went off and Nag was no more. Teddy's father had heard the noise and now he had shot the wicked snake.

"Thank you!" he cried. "You saved our lives."

Rikki-Tikki-Tavi felt very pleased with himself, but he knew he still had to deal with Nagaina.

The next day he ran into the yard.

"Darzee, I need you to distract Nagaina for me," he cried.

As soon as the coast was clear, Rikki-Tikki-Tavi rushed to the cobra's nest and began to smash the eggs. He had just picked up the last egg when Darzee started to scream.

"Quick, Rikki-Tikki-Tavi!" he cried. "Nagaina is going to hurt Teddy!"

Rikki-Tikki-Tavi rushed up to the house. Nagaina was coiled, ready to strike Teddy.

"Stop!" shouted Rikki-Tikki-Tavi. "I've smashed all your eggs. This is the last one."

Nagaina sprang at the mongoose. She snatched the egg and rushed into her burrow.

Rikki-Tikki-Tavi just had time to grab her tail. He followed her into the dark burrow.

Darzee held his breath. "Oh, this is not good."

But a few minutes later, the mongoose appeared.

"It's all over," he said proudly. "The cobras are dead."

"You saved our lives again!" cried Teddy's mother.

And that's the last time a cobra ever dared set foot inside the walls of Rikki-Tikki Tavi's yard!

The Smallest Knight

Frederick lived in the royal castle, just like all the Queen's knights. Every day, he joined in with the parades and watched all the jousting games. Every night, he dreamed of being one of the Queen's knights.

"I know I could be a good knight," he said. But Frederick wasn't a knight. He was a servant boy. And nobody had ever heard of a servant boy being made a knight.

One day, Frederick was trying on a knight's helmet when the Queen came in, followed by all her knights.

"The key to the kingdom has been lost," she said. "Without it, nothing will work properly. It must be found!"

"I will find the key," said Frederick, nervously piping up.

The other knights didn't know who he was. "You're much too small to be a real knight," they said, laughing.

But the Queen nodded at Frederick. "You can help my knights search for the key. If you find it, I will make you a knight," she said.

The knights crawled through fields and climbed trees. They dived into lakes and peered under bushes. But none of them found the key.

At the end of the day, weary and glum, they rode back to the castle. "Your key has vanished forever," they told the Queen.

"Nonsense!" cried a voice. Frederick strode forward and held up a shining key. "It had slipped through a crack in the castle floorboards," he said. "Sometimes it helps to be small!"

"You have saved the day," cried the Queen. "Thank you. I will keep my promise to you."

Smiling, the Queen lifted her golden sword and touched Frederick on each shoulder.

"Arise, Sir Frederick," she said.

Everyone cheered. From now on, they knew that even a small servant could become an heroic knight!

Sippity, Sippity Sup

Sippity sup, sippity sup,
Bread and milk from a china cup.
Bread and milk from a bright silver spoon
Made of a piece of the bright silver moon.
Sippity sup, sippity sup,
Sippity, sippity sup.

Eeper Weeper

Eeper Weeper, chimney sweeper,
Married a wife and could not keep her.
Married another,
Did not love her,
Up the chimney he did shove her!

Old King Cole

Old King Cole was a merry old soul,
And a merry old soul was he;
He called for his pipe, and he called for his bowl,
And he called for his fiddlers three.

Little Blue Ben

Little Blue Ben, who lives in the glen,
Keeps a blue cat and one blue hen,
Which lays of blue eggs a score and ten;
Where shall I find the little Blue Ben?

Hannah Bantry

Hannah Bantry,
In the pantry,
Gnawing on a mutton bone;
How she gnawed it,
How she clawed it,
When she found herself alone.

Dame Trot

Dame Trot and her cat
Sat down for a chat;
The dame sat on this side
And puss sat on that.
"Puss," says the dame,
"Can you catch a rat,
Or a mouse in the dark?"
"Purr," says the cat.

The Cunning Hare and the Lion

There was once a powerful lion who ruled the jungle. He was cruel and killed the other animals whenever he felt like it. The animals had had enough, so they went to the lion's den.

"O, Master, you kill many of us every day without need," they cried. "One animal a day is enough to satisfy your hunger. Please come to an agreement with us. Starting from today, we promise to offer one among us to you every day. In this way, you will not have to hunt and many of our lives will be spared."

The lion thought about this for a moment. "I agree," he said, "but if I do not receive an animal every day, I will kill all of you!"

With this agreement in place, the animals happily went about their business, and only one unlucky creature was sent to the lion each day.

One day, a hare was chosen. But he didn't want to become the lion's dinner, so he came up with a clever plan.

The hare waited until the evening before visiting the lion's den.

"You have made me wait all day for my dinner!" roared the lion. "I will eat you and then kill all the other animals."

"O, Master, don't do that," pleaded the hare. "I can explain. On the way here I met another lion who said he was the king of the jungle, and that we should only offer ourselves as food to him. He says you are an imposter."

On hearing this, the lion was furious. "Take me to this pretender. I will show him who's king of the jungle!"

The hare led the lion to a well.

"Sir, the lion lives in that den down there," said the hare. The lion looked into the well and saw his own reflection. He thought it was the other lion. With a mighty roar he leapt into the well—and that was the end of him!

The hare was given a hero's celebration for his cleverness. And from then on, the animals lived happily in peace in the jungle.

The Musicians of Bremen

Once upon a time, a farmer had a donkey. The animal had worked hard for him for many long years, but now he was old and unfit.

"You work too slowly," said the farmer. "I don't want you any more." And he sent the donkey away.

Although the donkey felt sad, he decided to make the most of his freedom. He had always wanted to be a musician, so he set off for the town of Bremen to start his new career.

He hadn't walked far when he found a dog lying on the road, panting hard.

"What's wrong, my friend?" asked the donkey.

"My master sent me away because I am old and weak and can no longer hunt," puffed the dog. "But how can an old mutt like me earn a living?"

"Why don't you join me," said the donkey. "I'm going to Bremen to become a musician."

The dog agreed to go with the donkey and they set off to town together.

After they had walked a short distance, they saw a cat. She was meowing sorrowfully.

"What's wrong?" asked the donkey. "You sound so sad."

"My mistress has sent me away because I'm too old to catch mice any more."

"Come with us to Bremen," said the donkey. "You sing beautifully and will make a fine musician."

The cat thought it sounded like a splendid idea and decided to join them.

It was getting dark when they met a cockerel, crowing mournfully with all his might.

"What's wrong?" asked the donkey.

"My master wanted to give me to the butcher," cried the cockerel. "So I ran away."

"Come with us. We're off to town to become musicians. You can sing with us," said the donkey.

247

The four friends carried on down the road. It was late at night when they came to a little cottage on the edge of the forest. They were tired and hungry, so they decided to see if they could shelter there for the night.

They went to the window and peered in. Sitting around a table laden with food and money was a gang of thieves.

The friends knew the thieves would never share their food or shelter, so they thought up a clever plan for getting rid of them.

The donkey put his front hooves on the window ledge. The dog jumped on his back. The cat climbed on the dog's back. And, last of all, the cockerel perched upon the cat's head. Then, in their loudest voices, they began to sing, before bursting through the window. The thieves, who thought that some terrible monster had come for them, ran away into the forest as fast as they could.

Laughing, the four friends sat down at the table and ate all the delicious food. Then, after such a long and exciting day, as they were all very tired, they turned out the lights and searched for a bed.

The donkey lay down on some straw in the yard.

The dog lay on the mat beside the door.

The cat curled up in front of the fire.

And the cockerel perched on top of the chimney.

The four friends were very happy to have found a new home, so they decided to stay in the cottage.

I expect that they are still there now, and if you stand outside their windows, you'll probably hear them practicing their singing!

The Noisy Dinosaur!

Toby T. Rex was feeling sad. The other dinosaurs didn't want to hang out with him any more. They said he was just too noisy and too clumsy. But he was a big dinosaur, and big dinosaurs were meant to be noisy and stomp and crash around, weren't they ...?

Toby's roar was so loud that it blew the leaves off the trees and Mrs. Triceratops' clean washing right off the line into the muddy swamp.

His huge feet were so stompy that, when he walked through the forest, the earth trembled and trees crashed to the ground.

When he played dino football, he left huge craters in the field.

Day after day, all Toby heard was,

"TOBY! Please be quiet!"

"Oh, Toby, now look what you've done!"

With a loud sigh and a big crash, Toby sat under a tall tree.

"If only I wasn't so clumsy and noisy!" he cried loudly. "No one likes me!"

Toby's sobs got louder and louder.

"Toby, don't cry," soothed Mrs. Triceratops. "Of course we like you. But just because you're big it doesn't mean you have to stomp and roar at the top of your voice. And if you move more slowly you won't knock things over."

"Really? I think I can try that," sniffed Toby. Slowly he stood up and took a few small steps. No trees crashed to the ground.

"Oh, look!" Toby whispered using his softest voice. "It works!"

The other dinosaurs smiled.

Toby grinned and took a few more steps on his tiptoes.

"I can do it!" he said using a small voice. "It's not so hard ..."

CRASH!

"Oops!" Toby roared loudly, as he tripped over his own feet.

Everyone laughed.

"Oh, Toby!" sighed Mrs. Triceratops, smiling. "I think it's going to take some practice, but you'll get there in the end!"

From Wibbleton to Wobbleton

From Wibbleton to Wobbleton
is fifteen miles,
From Wobbleton to Wibbleton
is fifteen miles,
From Wibbleton to Wobbleton,
From Wobbleton to Wibbleton,
From Wibbleton to Wobbleton
is fifteen miles.

Hark! Hark!

Hark! Hark!
The dogs do bark,
Beggars are coming to town:
Some in rags,
Some in tags,
And some in velvet gowns.

Handy Spandy

Handy Spandy, Jack-a-dandy
Loved plum cake and sugar candy;
He bought some at a grocer's shop,
And out he came, hop, hop, hop.

250

Seesaw, Sacradown

Seesaw, Sacradown,
Which is the way to London Town?
One foot up and one foot down,
That's the way to London Town.

The House that Jack Built

This is the house that Jack built.
This is the man all tattered and torn,
That kissed the maiden all forlorn,
That milked the cow with the crumpled horn,
That tossed the dog,
That worried the cat,
That killed the rat,
That ate the malt
That lay in the house that Jack built.

If Wishes Were Horses

If wishes were horses,
Beggars would ride;
If turnips were watches,
I'd wear one by my side.

251

Up in my Airplane

Archie was an excellent pilot and he loved flying. Each night, he dreamed of flying around the world. Every morning, he jumped into his airplane and zoomed up among the clouds.

"Wheee!" he shouted, looping the loop. "This is the best feeling in the world!" There was only one problem. His flying adventures never lasted long enough! School and homework always got in the way. So one weekend, Archie decided to make his dreams come true.

"I'm going on an adventure," he said. "This weekend, I'm going to fly farther than I've ever flown before."

Archie packed some food and a change of clothes, and climbed into his airplane. His mom and dad and sister waved to him from the ground, as his airplane shot up into the sky.

"Look out, world," he shouted. "Here we come!"

In the distance, Archie could
see the ocean sparkling in the
moonlight. "I wonder if there are any pirates
at sea," he said. The airplane flew out over the
foamy waves. Soon he spotted a ship cutting through
the water. A Jolly Roger flag fluttered from the highest mast and
a pirate sat in the lookout. Archie waved from his airplane.

"Look out, me hearties!" the pirate roared. "A flying pirate!"

The pirates aimed their cannons at the airplane, but Archie
was miles away before they could fire!

Archie zoomed over playful dolphins, leaping fish, and giant
octopuses. He saw desert islands with palm trees waving in the
breeze. Then he reached land again, and zoomed over cities,
towns, and fields, until he saw a fairground.

"Awesome!" Archie cried. He landed his airplane and ran off
to explore. There were lots of rides, but something was missing.

"There's no Ferris wheel!" said a little girl sadly. "I want to go
up high."

Archie smiled. "I've got an idea," he said.

He went back to his airplane.

"Roll up!" he shouted in his loudest voice.
"Free rides on the best little airplane in the world!"

Soon there was a line of
people stretching all around
the fairground, waiting for
a ride on the little airplane.
Archie gave everyone a ride,
and when the fairground closed,
he flew on until he came to the highest
mountains he had ever seen. They were topped
with snow, and the sun was dazzling. Archie
spiraled around the mountaintops.

"They look like ice cream," he said. "This is
making me hungry!"

Just then, Archie spotted a little café at the very
top of the highest mountain. He landed his airplane
and ordered a hot chocolate with marshmallows and
sprinkles. The sun was setting and the stars were starting to
twinkle. Archie yawned.

"Maybe it's time to go home," he said. But he had been flying
for so long that he couldn't remember the way. "I wish I'd
brought a map. Come on, little airplane. Let's just keep flying
and see what we find."

In his little airplane, Archie zoomed over a busy city.
"I recognize these streets," he said. Then he saw some people waving at him. It was his mom, dad, and sister. Archie had flown all the way around the world until he arrived back home!

The Queen of Hearts

The Queen of Hearts, she made some tarts,
All on a summer's day;
The Knave of Hearts, he stole the tarts,
And took them clean away.
The King of Hearts called for the tarts,
And beat the Knave full sore;
The Knave of Hearts brought back the tarts,
And vowed he'd steal no more.

Washing Up

When I was a little boy
I washed my mommy's dishes;
I put my finger in one eye,
And pulled out golden fishes.

Rain Before Seven

Rain before seven,
Fine by eleven.

Cobbler, Cobbler

Cobbler, cobbler, mend my shoe,
Get it done by half past two;
Stitch it up, and stitch it down,
Then I'll give you half a crown.

What's the News?

"What's the news of the day,
Good neighbor, I pray?"
"They say the balloon
Is gone up to the moon."

King Arthur

When famed King Arthur ruled this land
He was a goodly king:
He took three pecks of barley meal
To make a bag pudding.
A rare pudding the king did make,
And stuffed it well with plums;
And in it put such lumps of fat,
As big as my two thumbs.
The king and queen did eat thereof,
And noblemen beside,
And what they could not eat that night
The queen next morning fried.

Dick Whittington and his Cat

Once upon a time there was a poor orphan boy, named Dick Whittington, who lived in a little village in the countryside. He was often very hungry. He had heard tales about a faraway place called London, where everyone was rich and the streets were paved with gold, so he decided to set off for this wonderful place.

But when he arrived in London, there was no gold to be seen anywhere.

Disappointed and hungry, poor Dick slumped onto the steps of a rich merchant's house. The mean cook that worked there tried to shoo him away, but the merchant was a kind man and he took pity on Dick. He gave him a job working in the kitchen. Even though the cook was mean to him, and he had to sleep in a small room full of rats and mice, Dick was very grateful to the kind merchant.

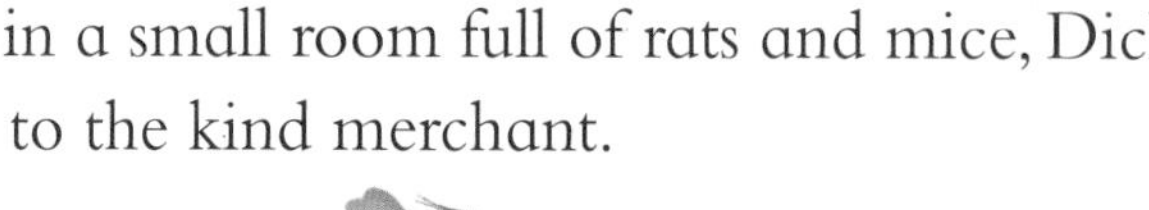

Dick saved up all his pennies and bought a cat to kill the rats and mice. After this, his life was much easier and he could sleep at night.

One day, the merchant, who was setting off on a voyage to the other side of the world, asked his household if anyone had anything they wanted him to take on his ship so that he could sell it for them. The only thing Dick had was his cat, so he asked him to take it.

"I will see what I can get for it," said the merchant.

And the kind merchant was true to his word. He sold Dick's cat to a king and queen who had a terrible rat problem in their palace. They were so pleased with the cat, they gave the merchant a ship full of gold, which he passed on to Dick.

Dick was never hungry or poor again. He used his money wisely. He never forgot his kind friend the merchant, and when he grew up he married the merchant's daughter, and they all lived happily ever after.

Clap, Clap Hands

Clap, clap hands, one, two, three,
Put your hands upon your knees,
Lift them up high to touch the sky,
Clap, clap hands and away they fly.

Head, Shoulders, Knees, and Toes

Head, shoulders, knees, and toes, knees, and toes,
Head, shoulders, knees, and toes, knees, and toes,
And eyes and ears and mouth and nose.
Head, shoulders, knees, and toes, knees, and toes.

My Hands

My hands upon my head I place,
On my shoulders, on my face.

On my hips I place them so,
Then bend down to touch my toe.

Now I raise them up so high,
Make my fingers fairly fly.

Now I clap them, one, two, three.
Then I fold them silently.

Two Little Men

Two little men in a flying saucer
Flew round the world one day.
They looked left and right,
And they didn't like the sight,
So then they flew away!

I Met a Man

As I was going up the stair
I met a man who wasn't there.
He wasn't there again today—
Oh how I wish he'd go away!

Ten Little Men

Ten little men standing straight,
Ten little men open the gate,
Ten little men all in a ring,
Ten little men bow to the king,
Ten little men dance all day,
Ten little men hide away.

Little Elephant's Clever Trick

Little Elephant set off for a walk. Today he wanted to explore. He hadn't gone far when he met Zebra.

Little Elephant had never seen a zebra before. He looked at Zebra's cool stripes. Then he looked at his own plain skin. Little Elephant was puzzled.

"Excuse me," Little Elephant said. "Why are you stripy?"

"So I can hide," replied Zebra. "When I'm in the grass, out on the plain, it's really hard to see me. I'll show you!"

He galloped off. Little Elephant tried to see where he went, but Zebra had disappeared.

Little Elephant was amazed. "You're right! It is hard to see you. That's so clever."

Little Elephant wandered on. Before long, Little Elephant met Giraffe. He had never seen a giraffe before.

Little Elephant looked at Giraffe's pretty patches. Then he looked at his own gray skin.

"Excuse me," Little Elephant said. "Why are you covered in patches?"

"So I can hide," Giraffe replied. "When I'm under the trees and the sun's shining, it's really hard to see me. I'll show you!"

Giraffe walked over to some trees. Little Elephant tried to see where she went, but Giraffe had disappeared. Little Elephant was impressed.

"You're right! It is hard to see you. That's so clever."

Little Elephant was starting to feel very sad. "I can't hide anywhere," he thought. "Everyone would be able to see me. I wish I was like Zebra or Giraffe."

He knelt down, bowed his head, and began to cry.

Giraffe and Zebra came back with Crocodile. "Where's Little Elephant?" asked Giraffe. "He was here a minute ago."

"Well, he's not here now," said Zebra. "There's just that old rock over there."

The rock began to giggle. "It's me!" called Little Elephant. "I'm not a rock!"

"What a clever trick!" smiled Zebra.

"You don't need grass or trees," laughed Giraffe.

"You can hide anywhere, just like that," added Zebra.

"So I can," said Little Elephant.

"We came to see if you'd like to play," said Little Elephant's new friends.

"Yes, please!" replied Little Elephant. "I'd like to play hide-and-seek."

Underpants Thunderpants

One day when the weather is sunny and fine,
Dog hangs his underpants out on the line.
But thunder and lightning soon fill up the sky.
Underpants Thunderpants!
Look at them fly!
Over the ocean, the jungle and town—
Where will those undies come fluttering down?

"How odd," says the submarine captain below.
"First I saw lightning and now I see snow!"
Octopus wriggles and jiggles with glee.
"Four pairs of underpants perfect for me!"

Underpants Plunderpants!
Just imagine that!
Roger the Pirate has got a new hat!

Elephant's trunk has been tickled by bees.
"Oh bother!" he grumbles. "I'm going to sneeze,
But I don't have a tissue. What shall I do?
A jumbo-sized hankie! How handy!
ACHOO!"

Watch it! A hunter is out on the snoop.
Underpants Blunderpants!
Splat in the poop!

Up at the palace, the king says,
"Oh my! Three pairs of underpants
baked in a pie!"

A two-headed alien stares from his lair ...
"Underpants Wonderpants!
Now I'm not bare!"

267

Monsters Always

All mommies want their children to have good manners. But good monster manners are the opposite of good human manners.

"Mess up your toys," Mommy Monster said to Baby Monster each day. "Spill more food on the floor. Your hands are too clean!"

But Baby Monster just wanted to be neat and tidy.

"I'll take him to the park," said Daddy Monster. "Baby Monster will soon see how much fun it is to get messy!"

Daddy Monster took Baby Monster to the muddiest, slimiest pond in the park. "Let's collect water weeds!" he said. SQUELCH! They waded in and threw mud at each other.

"What a good little monster!" said the passersby.

Next, Daddy Monster put a picnic rug on the soggiest grass he could find. He opened the picnic hamper. "Tuck in, Baby Monster!" he said.

What a messy picnic! Squashy, ripe peaches dribbled down their chins. Cream puffs exploded over their faces. Sticky honey sandwiches stuck to their fur. Daddy Monster blew bubbles in the chocolate milkshake and drenched them both.

Giggling, Baby Monster jumped on Daddy Monster and gave him a big tickle. They rolled around in the soggy grass and fell into a bog with a big, squelchy PLOP! Daddy Monster felt very happy that Baby Monster had finally learned some good monster manners. But then,

"I want to go home now," said Baby Monster.

"So you can roll around and make the carpet muddy?" asked Daddy Monster.

"No," said Baby Monster, laughing. "So I can take a bath and get clean again!"

Oh no!

The Ant and the Grasshopper

One sunny day, a grasshopper was hopping and chirping happily in a field. An ant passed by, carrying food to his nest.

"Come and play with me," cried the grasshopper. "It's too hot to work. You can gather food some other day."

"I'm gathering food now for the winter," replied the ant. "There will be no food then. You should do the same."

"Don't be silly!" laughed the grasshopper. "There'll be plenty!"

The seasons changed. It grew cold and started to rain. Grasshopper was hungry. Shivering and wet, he hopped from place to place looking for something to eat.

Then he met the ant again. Ant was having his dinner.

"Where did you get that food?" cried the grasshopper.

"I gathered it when the sun was shining," replied the ant.

The grasshopper felt sad. "You were right," he sighed. "I should have gathered some food when I had the chance."

And the moral of the story is: It's best to be prepared for hard days ahead.

Two Men and the Bear

One day two men were walking through the forest when they came across a bear. Both men were scared. One man scampered up a nearby tree to hide. The other man wasn't quick enough. He knew there was nothing he could do to escape, so he dropped to the ground and pretended to be dead.

The bear came over to the man on the ground and sniffed him around his ears. The man was terrified, but the bear walked away.

As soon as the bear had gone, the other man jumped down from his hiding place.

"What did the bear say to you?" he asked.

"It said I should think about whether you're really my friend," the man answered. "You only cared about yourself and jumped in the tree without a thought for me!"

And the moral of the story is: Friendship is tested in times of trouble.

Pirates on the Plank

One morning, Erik the pirate captain woke up feeling really grumpy.

"I'm fed up with searching for treasure and never finding it," he said. "Being a pirate is no fun any more!"

Erik wondered if a few games might bring the fun back. He ordered his crew to start playing. They tried Tiddlywinks, Checkers, and Fish, but it was no use.

"You're all cheating!" Erik roared. "You no-good pirates. I don't want games! I want treasure and ships to sink!"

"Pieces of eight!" squawked his parrot.

"Yo ho ho!" shouted the pirates.

Then Erik had a bright idea. "I know what will cheer me up," he said to himself. "I'll make every single silly pirate walk the plank!"

SPLASH! One by one, the pirates stomped down the plank and jumped into the sea. SPLASH! Erik felt better already.

"We'll teach him a lesson!" the pirates spluttered, gathering together in the water.

The pirates climbed up a rope that hung over the side of the ship. Erik was standing beside the plank and singing.

"Ha ha ha!" he chortled. "They all made a silly splash! Ho ho ho!"

The pirates tiptoed up behind him. On the first mate's signal, they all shouted "BOO!"

Erik let out a yell of surprise and tumbled off the plank. SPLASH!

Giggling, the other pirates jumped off the plank too, dive bombing into the water with their captain. Erik spluttered and laughed as they splashed each other. All Erik's grumpy feelings disappeared. "Yo ho ho!" he shouted. "The life of a pirate is the best fun ever!"

Jack and the Beanstalk

There was once a young boy named Jack, who lived with his mother. They had no money and nothing left to eat.

"We have no choice but to sell Bluebell, our old cow," said Jack's mother. "Take her to market and sell her for a good price."

So Jack set off with Bluebell.

Before long, he met an old man, who asked, "Are you selling that fine cow?"

"Yes," Jack replied.

"Well, I'll give you these magic beans for her," said the man. "They don't look much, but if you plant them, you will soon be rich!"

Jack liked the sound of that, and he gave Bluebell to the man.

When Jack showed his mother the beans she was very angry.

"Silly boy! Go to your room!" she cried, throwing the beans out of the window.

The next morning, when Jack woke up, his room was strangely dark. He looked out of his window and saw a plant so tall that he couldn't see the top of it.

"It must be a magic beanstalk!" he cried.

Jack started to climb. When he reached the top, he saw a giant house. Jack's tummy was rumbling with hunger, so he knocked on the enormous door and a giant woman answered.

"Please may I have some breakfast?" asked Jack.

"You'll BE breakfast if my husband sees you!" said the woman.

But Jack begged and pleaded, and at last the giant's wife let him in. She gave him some bread and milk and hid him in a cupboard.

Soon Jack heard loud footsteps and felt the cupboard shake.

"Fee-fi-fo-fum! I smell the blood of an Englishman!" roared the giant.

"Don't be silly," the giant's wife said. "You smell the sausages I've cooked for your breakfast."

When the giant had finished eating, he counted the hundreds of huge gold coins in his treasure chest. But the counting soon sent him to sleep.

As quick as a flash, Jack grabbed the coins, ran out of the house and climbed down the beanstalk.

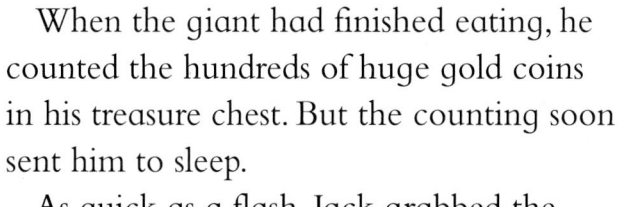

His mother was so happy to see the gold. "Clever boy! We'll never be poor again!" she laughed.

But soon Jack and his mother had spent all the money, so the boy climbed the beanstalk again. He knocked on the huge door and begged the giant's wife to give him some food. At last she let him in.

After eating his breakfast, Jack hid in the cupboard just as the giant arrived home for lunch.

When he had finished eating, his wife brought him his pet hen.

"Lay!" he bellowed, and the hen laid a golden egg. It laid ten eggs before the giant started to snore. Jack couldn't believe his luck, so he picked up the hen and ran.

His mother beamed when she saw the hen lay a golden egg.

"We will never be hungry again," she said.

But even though Jack and his mother were rich, the boy decided to climb the beanstalk one more time.

Jack knew the giant's wife wouldn't be happy to see him, so he sneaked in when she wasn't looking and hid in the cupboard.

When the giant came home, his wife brought him his
magic harp.

"Play!" he roared, and the harp played such sweet music
the giant soon fell asleep.

Jack saw his chance and grabbed the harp. As he ran,
the harp cried out, "Master! Help!"

The giant woke up and began to chase Jack down
the beanstalk.

"Mother, fetch the ax!" Jack yelled as he reached the ground.
He chopped at the beanstalk with all his might. CREAK!
GROAN! The giant quickly climbed back to
the top just before the beanstalk crashed to the ground.

When his mother heard the harp play, she
laughed and hugged Jack tightly.

"My clever boy!" she said. And the
two of them lived happily ever after.

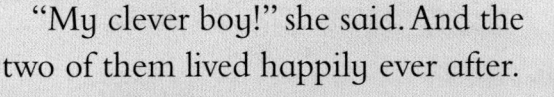

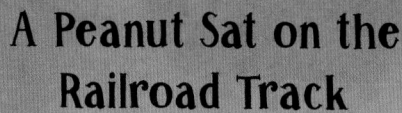

A Peanut Sat on the Railroad Track

A peanut sat on the railroad track,
His heart was all a-flutter;
Along came a train—the 9:15—
Toot, toot, peanut butter!

The Man in the Moon

The man in the moon
Came tumbling down,
And asked his way to Norwich.
He went by the south,
And burned his mouth
With supping cold pease-porridge.

Curly Locks

Curly Locks! Curly Locks! Wilt thou be mine?
Thou shalt not wash dishes, nor yet feed the swine,
But sit on a cushion and sew a fine seam,
And feed upon strawberries, sugar, and cream!

Michael Finnegan

There was an old man called Michael Finnegan
He grew whiskers on his chinnegan
The wind came out and blew them in again
Poor old Michael Finnegan. *Begin again ...*

Old Betty Blue

Old Betty Blue
Lost a holiday shoe,
What can old Betty do?
Give her another
To match the other,
And then she may swagger in two.

Little Nancy Etticoat

Little Nancy Etticoat, in a white petticoat,
And a red rose.
The longer she stands,
The shorter she grows.

What is she? A candle!

279

Farmyard Chase

Mother Hen sat on her nest and shook out her soft, fluffy feathers. She had an egg to keep warm. She had been sitting there for hours.

"I'm hungry," thought Mother Hen.

Suddenly, Mother Hen saw a patch of sunlight by the barn door. She had an idea. She rolled her egg carefully over into the sun and packed some hay round it. "That will keep you warm," she said. "I won't be long."

And off she went to find some corn.

Horse came trotting up to the barn. He was hungry, too. He saw the hay by the barn door.

"Yummy!" he neighed, as he pushed his velvety muzzle into the hay. Bump! Horse's nose nudged Mother Hen's egg.

The egg rocked, and then it rolled. It rolled across the yard.

"Oh no!" neighed Horse. The egg tumbled toward the apple tree.

Pig was snuffling around the apple tree as the egg rolled past his nose.

"Oh no!" squealed Pig. "Catch that egg before it cracks!" And he scampered after the egg as it tumbled into the grassy meadow.

Sheep was munching the tufty grass in the meadow as the egg rolled past her.

"Oh no!" bleated Sheep. "Catch that egg before it cracks!" And she skipped after the egg as it tumbled down the hill.

At the bottom of the hill, Cow was lying down, having a rest after lunch. Bump! The egg bounced against Cow's nose.

"Ouch!" mooed Cow. "What was that?" And she stared at the egg. Horse, Pig, and Sheep came running down the hill.

"Catch that egg before it cracks!" they called.

"I have caught it," replied Cow.

"My egg!" clucked Hen, flapping her way down the hill. Just then, there was a loud *Crack!*

"Someone must have cracked it!" clucked Hen. *Crack!* The crack got bigger still.

Suddenly, the egg cracked wide open. Out hopped a soft, fluffy ball of yellow feathers.

"It was me!" cheeped the little fluffy chick. "I cracked the egg all by myself!"

Warning

The robin and the redbreast,
The robin and the wren:
If you take them from their nest
You'll never thrive again.

Mr. East's Feast

Mr. East gave a feast;
Mr. North laid the cloth;
Mr. West did his best;
Mr. South burnt his mouth
With eating a hot potato.

Catch Him

Catch him, crow! Carry him, kite!
Take him away till the apples are ripe;
When they are ripe and ready to fall,
Here comes a baby, apples and all.

Wine and Cakes

Wine and cakes for gentlemen,
Hay and corn for horses,
A cup of ale for good old wives,
And kisses for the lasses.

The Little, Rusty, Dusty Miller

Oh the little, rusty, dusty miller,
Dusty was his coat,
Dusty was his color,
Dusty was the kiss
I got from the miller.
If I had my pockets
Full of gold and silver,
I would give it all
To my dusty miller.

Wee Willie Winkie

Wee Willie Winkie runs through the town,
Upstairs and downstairs in his nightgown,
Peeping through the keyhole, crying through the lock,
"Are the children in their beds? It's past eight o'clock!"

The Pirate King

The Pirate King was not happy. His ship had been attacked by another pirate ship. Even though the Pirate King and his crew had been outnumbered, they had fought bravely—but in the end, all his men had deserted him. Now he was alone with just his ship for company.

"How can I rule the ocean waves all by myself?" he sniffed, sailing toward a little desert island. "I'll stay here. I've got nothing else to do now."

But no pirate stays gloomy for long. "I belong on the ocean waves!" the Pirate King cried. "I'll be the crew *and* the captain of my own ship!" He jumped back on board, pulled on his pirate hat and set sail. With the Jolly Roger waving in the breeze, the Pirate King went to look for treasure and adventure.

A few days later, the Pirate King spotted another ship sailing toward him. He aimed all his cannons at it and ... BOOM! BOOM! BOOM!

"We surrender!" cried the sailors.

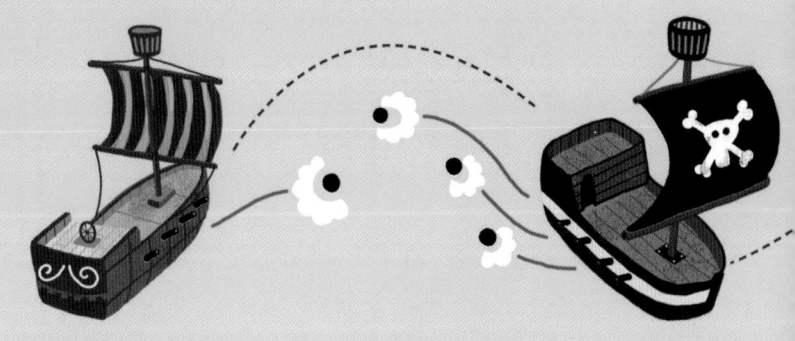

The Pirate King made them all walk the plank and then
took their treasure. There were chests filled with diamonds,
pearls, rubies, and coins. He stashed it aboard his boat and
then set sail for land, to bury his treasure.

At last he spotted an empty beach. It was perfect! The Pirate
King got to work. He grabbed his spade and started to dig.
Deeper and deeper he went. Then he buried his shining jewels
and coins and covered them over with sand.

"Now no other pirates can find my treasure," he said.
"Time for me to find a new crew."

The Pirate King set off in his ship. He'd only been sailing for
a couple of hours, when he spotted a man in ragged clothes
clinging to a broken piece of wood in the water.

"What happened to you?" asked the Pirate King.

"My ship sank," said the man. "Please help me!"

"Would you like to be the first mate on board a pirate ship,
under the command of a reckless and daring pirate king?" asked
the Pirate King.

The man nodded happily and clambered aboard the ship.

The Pirate King and his first mate sailed on, and they quickly filled the ship with pirates. But meanwhile, rumors of the Pirate King's treasure had spread to a town on the other side of the forest behind the empty beach. People started to search for the jewels and coins.

"Pirates love to bury their treasure," one man thought aloud. "If I dig a hole deep enough, I'm sure to find it!"

So, he got a spade, put on his hard hat and started to dig. He dug a hole so deep and long that it went under the town, under the forest and toward the beach. He dug and dug, and at last he broke through the golden sand of the beach. But when he climbed out of his hole, he got a big surprise. The Pirate King was standing there glaring at him!

The beach was filled with pirates, and their cutlasses glittered in the sunshine. They roared when they saw the man.

"Look out, me hearties! Thief! Make him walk the plank!" shouted the Pirate King.

The man was terrified. Before the pirates could grab him, he jumped back into the hole, and ran back home, along the tunnel he had made under the forest and the town.

"I'll never mess with pirates again!" he cried.

The Pirate King dug up his treasure, and then he and all his pirates climbed aboard the ship.

"Pull up the anchor!" shouted the Pirate King. "Now I've got my crew and my treasure, I can rule the ocean waves again!"

The Vain Monk

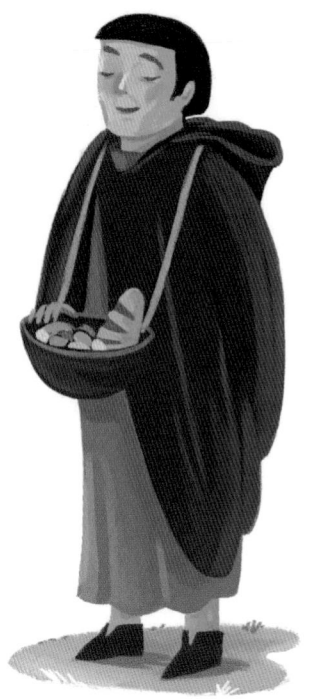

A long time ago, there was a proud monk. He wandered from town to town, seeking gifts of food and money. He had a great knowledge of his holy books and thought he knew more than everyone he met on his travels.

"These people are lucky that I am coming to ask them for gifts," he said when he reached the next town.

As was usual, when the townsfolk saw the monk walking along the street with his wooden bowl, they gave him generous gifts of food and money.

However, the vain monk never bothered to thank them. He thought it was his right because he was so clever.

"I'm so good, everyone can see the greatness in me!" he boasted.

When he got to the edge of the town, he saw a field full of rams. The monk walked into the field toward a huge ram. It lowered its big, sharp horns and began pawing the ground.

"Oh, look!" sighed the monk happily. "Even the animals know how great I am. See how this ram is bowing down to me."

The owner of the rams heard these silly, vain words. He called out to the monk, "Sir! Please be careful. The ram isn't bowing, he's about to attack you!"

"What nonsense!" snapped the monk. "Your ram can see my greatness!"

He had barely finished uttering these ridiculous words, when the ram charged at the monk.

The monk tried to run away, but it was too late. The ram butted him into the air. He fell with a hard bump and dropped his bowl of food.

"Oh, help me!" he cried. "I think I've broken a bone in my leg, and all my food is spoiled!"

"I'm sorry to say it, but you should have listened to me," said the man.

The monk hung his head in shame. "You are right. I'm sorry, I should not have been so vain."

"Well, I think you have learned your lesson now," smiled the man. "Come and have supper at my home."

And from that day on, the monk was never vain again, and he humbly thanked everyone that gave him gifts.

Tiger Footprints

It was a very hot day in the jungle. Tiggy and Mac were playing near the waterfall.

"Wheee!" shouted Tiggy, as she slid on the wet rocks.

Mac was watching a funny-looking frog. It croaked loudly and then hopped away.

"Where are you going?" asked Mac.

When the little frog didn't answer, Mac ran after it.

"Wait for me!" cried Tiggy.

The twins chased the frog through the leafy jungle.

"Look!" shouted Mac suddenly. Tiggy tumbled to a stop behind him. In front of them sat a whole family of funny-looking frogs.

"The little frog was hopping back home," said Mac.

Tiggy was tired after their long chase. "I want to go home," she groaned.

Mac looked around. They had never been here before. He didn't know how to get home.

"I wish Mom were here," sighed Mac. "She always knows the way home."

As the two cubs looked around, Tiggy noticed a trail of footprints on the soft jungle floor. The footprints were round—and very big.

"Maybe they'll lead us home," said Mac.

The little tigers followed them carefully, and at the end of the trail, they came across a baby elephant.

"This isn't home," said Tiggy. And the two cubs ran away as fast as their little legs could carry them. Finally, the little tigers had run far enough and they stopped for a rest.

"Look! We've made a trail, too," said Mac.

The pair looked back at the footprints that followed them.

"Let's make some more," cried Tiggy. And they ran faster and faster, making a zigzagging trail of tiger footprints.

Then Tiggy noticed some more footprints nearby.

"Those look just like ours," she said, "but much bigger."

"Mom!" they both shouted together.

And the little cubs began to follow the big tiger footprints back through the leafy jungle to where...

... Mom stood waiting.

"Come on, you two little tigers," she said, smiling at her cubs. "Time to go home!"

Scaredy Squirrel

Every day, Ollie the squirrel would jump out at his sister Annabel and scare her.

"Stop it!" she said one day. "I don't like being surprised."

But Ollie thought it was just a bit of fun. So Annabel decided to show him how it felt. She hid behind a big tree until Ollie came along.

"BOO!" she shouted. Ollie gave a yell and scampered up to the top of the tree.

"That wasn't very nice," he said.

"You always say that being scared is just a bit of fun," Annabel said.

Suddenly, Ollie understood how he had made Annabel feel.

"I'm very sorry," he said. "Will you forgive me?"

"Of course I will," said Annabel.

"I know where there is a secret stash of nuts," said Ollie. "Want to share them with me?"

"That's the kind of surprise I love!" said Annabel. "Let's go!"

The River Rapid Race

Max and Alice were otters who loved adventure. One day, they found two hollow logs bobbing by the riverbank.

"Let's race each other!" said Alice. "Bet I'm faster!"

They jumped into the wooden logs and whooshed downstream. At first Max was in the lead, but Alice soon bumped past him.

Faster and faster they both went, and the logs bobbed and wobbled! They weaved between big rocks and water sprayed all around them. Suddenly ... CRASH! Alice's log hit a rock. It turned over and she splashed into the rushing river. Max reached for his friend's paw and pulled her onto his log. They shot out of the rapids and into a calmer part of the river.

"It's a tie!" Max cheered as they bobbed to the bank. "That was super-scary—and super-cool!"

Anansi and His Sons

Anansi and his wife, Aso, had six sons. They were called See Trouble, Road Builder, River Drinker, Animal Skinner, Stone Thrower, and Cushion!

One day Anansi had to go on a long journey. On his trip, he found a big, bright, glowing ball. He was carrying this special object home when he accidentally fell into a lake and was swallowed whole by a huge fish.

Anansi started to shout for help. "If I am lucky enough to be rescued," he thought, "I will give my rescuer this glowing ball."

When Anansi didn't return home, his sons became very worried. See Trouble saw a vision of his father inside the big fish. He told his brothers.

"I will clear a path through the jungle to the lake," said Road Builder, and they all set off.

When they got to the lake, River Drinker drank all the water in the lake. Lying on the mud at the bottom of the lake was the big fish.

Animal Skinner immediately cut open the fish and let Anansi out. Anansi was just about to thank his sons, when a large bird swooped out of the sky and grabbed him. Stone Thrower grabbed a rock and threw it at the bird.

Down, down, down, fell Anansi. Cushion lay on the ground and Anansi had a soft landing.

Anansi wanted to give the glowing ball to the son who had rescued him, but he couldn't decide which son had done the most to help him.

Instead, he gave the glowing object to Nyame, the Sky God, and he put this Moon up in the sky. We can still see it now because Anansi never figured out which son deserved it the most!

Mowgli's Brothers

As the sun set over the jungle, the Wolf family stirred in their cave. Father Wolf prepared to go hunting, while Mother Wolf watched over her four playful cubs.

As Father Wolf left the cave, he heard a terrifying roar. It was Shere Khan the tiger, the most feared animal in the whole of the jungle. Suddenly, the bushes rustled and Father Wolf prepared to pounce. But it wasn't Shere Khan. It was a naked baby.

"A man cub!" gasped Father Wolf.

"Quick, bring him into the cave!" cried Mother Wolf. The baby snuggled up against Mother Wolf, just as Shere Khan appeared at the cave entrance.

"Give me the man cub," roared the huge tiger. "I've hunted him through the jungle and he's mine."

The wolves knew Shere Khan was too big to get into the cave so they stood their ground.

"No!" Mother Wolf shouted. "He will not be killed. We will bring him up with our cubs. Now go!"

The cowardly tiger knew he was no match for all the wolves working together. Slinking off back into the jungle, he cried, "We will see what the Pack Council has to say about you adopting a man cub."

"We will keep him," Mother Wolf declared. "And we will call him Mowgli."

At the next full moon, the Pack Council met to decide whether Mowgli could stay. Shere Khan arrived to try and persuade the wolves to hand over the man cub. Some of the younger wolves in the pack agreed with him, but Akela, the leader of the pack, spoke out.

"You all know the rules. If two people, other than his parents, can speak in favor of him, Mowgli can stay. Who speaks for this cub?" he cried.

"I speak for the man cub," said a loud voice. "I myself will watch out for him."

It was Baloo, the brown bear whose job it was to teach the wolf cubs the Law of the Jungle.

"Me too!" purred the soft voice of Bagheera, the black panther. Everyone knew the wise panther and all respected him.

"It's settled them," said Akela. "The man cub can stay. He may be a help to us one day."

Many years passed and Mowgli grew big and strong. He learned all about the jungle, and he ran and hunted with the pack. Sometimes Mowgli would creep down to the village and watch the people. He knew they were his kind, but he was happy with his wolf family and animal friends.

Shere Khan was biding his time. Bagheera knew that he would try and kill Mowgli one day.

And that day came soon enough, when Akela was too old and feeble to run the pack and protect Mowgli any more. The younger wolves wanted to hand Mowgli over to the ferocious tiger and they turned against Akela.

"Mowgli, run to the village," hissed Bagheera, "and fetch the Red Flower."

Bagheera was referring to fire. All the animals were scared of man's fire.

Mowgli returned to the pack waving a burning branch. They cowered in fear.

"If you let Akela go, I will go to the village and live among people."

Mowgli thrust the fire toward Shere Khan. "As for you," he shouted, "next time I see you, there will be trouble."

The cowardly tiger scampered away in fright.

With tears in his eyes, Mowgli said farewell to his wolf family.

"We will miss you," cried Mother Wolf.

"I'll visit," said Mowgli, before setting off to his new life.

Sneeze on Monday

Sneeze on Monday, sneeze for danger;
Sneeze on Tuesday, kiss a stranger;
Sneeze on Wednesday, get a letter;
Sneeze on Thursday, something better;
Sneeze on Friday, sneeze for sorrow;
Sneeze on Saturday, see your sweetheart tomorrow.

Bless You

Bless you, bless you, bonnie bee,
Tell me when my wedding be;
If it be tomorrow day,
Take your wings and fly away.
Fly to the east, fly to the west,
Fly to him I love the best.

One, Two

One, two, whatever you do,
Start it well and carry it through.
Try, try, never say die,
Things will come right,
You know, by and by.

Young Roger Came Tapping

Young Roger came tapping at Dolly's window,
Thumpaty, thumpaty, thump!
He asked for admittance, she answered him "No!"
Frumpaty, frumpaty, frump!
"No, no, Roger, no! As you came you may go!"
Stumpaty, stumpaty, stump!

Harry Parry

O rare Harry Parry,
When will you marry?
When apples and pears are ripe.
I'll come to your wedding,
Without any bidding,
And dance and sing all the night.

Apples, Peaches, Pears, and Plums

Apples, peaches,
pears, and plums,
Tell me when
your birthday comes.

I Love My Daddy

One day, Little Squirrel wanted to show Daddy Squirrel all the things he could do.

"What shall we do first?" said Daddy.

"Digging!" said Little Squirrel excitedly, as he dug and dug, with his little tail wagging.

"Well done!" said Daddy. But suddenly, Little Squirrel's tail stopped wagging.

"Help, Daddy! I'm stuck!"

Daddy Squirrel helped Little Squirrel wriggle out of the hole, and gave him a hug.

"You are a good digger!" said Daddy. "What shall we play next?"

"Climbing!" said Little Squirrel, and he climbed as high as he could go.

"Well done!" said Daddy. But suddenly Little Squirrel closed his eyes tightly …

"Help, Daddy! I'm stuck!"

Daddy Squirrel helped Little Squirrel climb down and gave him a hug.

"You are a good climber!" said Daddy. "What shall we play next?"

"Jumping!" said Little Squirrel, and he jumped with a big smile on his face. But suddenly Little Squirrel stopped smiling, and … SPLAT! He was in the mud.

"Help, Daddy! I'm stuck again!"

Daddy Squirrel helped Little Squirrel out of the sticky patch of mud and gave him a hug.

"You are good at jumping!" said Daddy.

But Little Squirrel shook his head sadly ...

"I can't do anything!" cried Little Squirrel. "I always get stuck!"

Daddy Squirrel lifted Little Squirrel on to his shoulders.

"Let's play together," he said. "Let's run!"

Little Squirrel held on tightly as they whooshed through the woods.

"Yippee!" he shouted.

"Let's climb!" said Daddy Squirrel. Little Squirrel kept his eyes open wide as they reached the top of a tree.

"Wheeee!" he shouted.

"And now," said Daddy Squirrel, "let's jump!"

SPLAT!

"Oh, help!" cried Daddy Squirrel. "Now I'm stuck!"

Little Squirrel giggled as he helped his daddy out of the sticky mud.

"You can do everything, Little Squirrel!" said Daddy proudly. "You can even save a Daddy Squirrel!"

Little Squirrel grinned. "I love playing with you ... and I love my daddy!" he shouted, and they raced home happily together.

Eat, Birds, Eat!

Eat, birds, eat, and make no waste;
I lie here and make no haste:
If my master chance to come,
You must fly, and I must run!

Once I Saw a Little Bird

Once I saw a little bird
Come hop, hop, hop;
So I cried, "Little bird,
Will you stop, stop, stop?"
I was going to the window,
To say, "How do you do?"
But he shook his little tail,
And far away he flew.

The Little Bird

This little bird flaps its wings,
Flaps its wings, flaps its wings,
This little bird flaps its wings,
And flies away in the morning!

Hickory Dickory Dock

Hickory dickory dock,
The mouse ran up the clock.
The clock struck one,
The mouse ran down,
Hickory dickory dock.

Marking Time

Tick! Tock!
That's the clock
Marking time for me.
Every tick
And every tock,
Sets each second free.

Old Mother Hubbard

Old Mother Hubbard
Went to the cupboard,
To get her poor doggie a bone.
But when she got there
The cupboard was bare,
And her poor little doggie had none.

The Three Little Pigs

Once upon a time, three little pigs lived together with their mother. One day it was time for them to leave home and build houses of their own.

"Be careful of the big, bad wolf," warned their mother as they trotted off down the road.

The first little pig built his house from straw.

Before long the big, bad wolf came to call.

"Little pig, little pig, let me come in," growled the wolf, licking his lips. He had come for his supper.

"Not by the hairs on my chinny-chin-chin!" the first little pig replied.

"Well, I'll huff and I'll puff and I'll blow your house down!" snarled the wolf. And that's just what he did. The little pig ran away as fast as he could.

The second little pig decided to build his house from sticks.

When the wolf saw the house, he pushed his nose against the door, and growled, "Little pig, little pig, let me come in."

"Not by the hairs on my chinny-chin-chin!" cried the second little pig.

"Well, I'll huff and I'll puff and I'll blow your house down!" snarled the wolf. And that's just what he did. The little pig ran away as fast as he could.

The third little pig built a strong house from bricks. He had just put a pot of soup on the fire to boil when he saw his brothers running down the path, closely followed by the wolf.

"Quick!" cried the third little pig. He opened the door and let his brothers inside.

"Little pigs, little pigs, let me come in!" roared the wolf.

"Not by the hairs on our chinny-chin-chins," cried the three little pigs.

"Well, I'll huff and I'll puff and I'll blow your house down!" snarled the wolf. So he huffed and he puffed ... And he huffed and he puffed ... But the house stood firm.

The wolf climbed onto the roof and slid down the chimney—straight into the pot of hot soup.

"Owwwoooo!" he cried.

The wolf leaped up and ran out of the house, never to be seen again!

Clever Jackal Gets Away

One day Jackal was trotting through a narrow, rocky pass, looking for something to eat, when he saw Lion coming toward him.

Jackal was filled with fear. He had played so many tricks on Lion in the past, he was sure that Lion wouldn't miss this opportunity to take his revenge. In a flash, Jackal thought of a cunning plan.

"Oh, great Lion—help!" he cried, looking up at the rocks above his head. "See that huge rock above us? It's about to fall and we shall both be crushed. Please save us!"

Lion looked up, in alarm.

"Don't worry," he cried. "I'm strong. I'll hold it up while you go for help!"

"Oh, thank you, great King!" yelped Jackal. "I will fetch that log over there to put under the rock!"

And with that, he ran away, leaving Lion holding the rock that wasn't going to fall at all!

Thunder and Lightning

A long time ago, Thunder and Lightning lived on Earth among the people.

Thunder was an old mother sheep, and Lightning was her only son, a ram. Whenever the ram got angry he would go on the rampage, knocking down trees and causing trouble. When he did these terrible things, his mother would shout at him to stop in a very loud, rumbling voice. But Lightning didn't listen. He still caused damage whenever he was in a bad mood.

At last the people of the land couldn't stand it any more, and they complained to their king.

The king banished both Thunder and Lightning from the Earth and made them live in the sky.

Lightning still gets angry and tries to cause destruction; that's why you can see light flashing across the sky in a storm. And Thunder continues to shout at him, her booming voice following after the flash of light.

Jack's next job was with a merchant, who gave him a donkey for his trouble. Jack was a strong lad, but he found it difficult to hoist the donkey on his shoulder. At last he managed and started to stagger home slowly.

Now it happened that in a house on his route home, there lived a rich man with his only daughter, a beautiful girl, who had not spoken for many years. The doctors said she would never recover her voice until somebody made her laugh. Her father had promised her in marriage to the first man who made her laugh.

As Jack staggered past the house, the girl happened to be looking out of the window. The sight of the donkey with its legs in the air was so comical and strange, the girl burst out laughing and immediately got her voice back. Her father was overjoyed and asked Jack to marry his daughter.

Jack and his mother were never poor again. They lived happily ever after in a large house with Jack's wife and her father.

Rumpelstiltskin

Long ago, a poor miller was so desperate to impress the king that he told him his daughter could spin straw into gold!

"This I must see," said the king.

The next day, at the palace, the king led the girl to a room filled with straw.

"Spin this into gold by morning," he demanded, then left.

The girl wept at the impossible task. Suddenly, a strange little man appeared.

"Give me your necklace and I will help you," he told her.

The girl handed it to him, and the strange little man sat in front of the spinning wheel and spun the straw into gold.

The next day, the delighted king took the miller's daughter to an even bigger room filled with straw.

"Spin this into gold and you shall be my queen!" he said.

The strange little man appeared once more, but the girl had nothing left to give him.

"If you become queen," he told her, "you can give me your first-born child."

The girl agreed. Once again, he spun the straw into gold.

The next day, the king married the miller's daughter, and the new queen soon forgot all about the strange little man.

A year passed and the queen had a bonny baby boy. It did not take long for the little man to appear again.

"Please don't take my son," the queen begged.

"If you guess my name you can keep your baby—you have three days," said the little man.

For two nights after that the little man would appear in the baby's nursery. The queen would try to guess his name, but all of her guesses were wrong.

On the morning of the third day, one of the queen's servants was in the forest chopping logs when he saw a funny little man leaping around a fire and singing. He hid behind a tree and listened:

The queen will never win my game,
For Rumpelstiltskin is my name!

The servant hurried home to tell the queen.

That night, when the queen correctly guessed the little man's name, he was furious. He turned red with rage and ran off into the forest, never to be seen again.

The Man Who Never Lied

Once upon a time, there lived a wise man named Mamad. He never told lies. He was famous throughout the land for his wisdom and honesty.

The king had heard about Mamad. He decided to test the wise man's honesty for himself. So one morning, as he got ready to go hunting, he called the wise man to his side. With his left foot on the horse's stirrup, the king turned to Mamad.

"Go to my summer palace and tell the queen I will be with her for lunch. Tell her to prepare a big feast. You will then have lunch with me."

Mamad bowed to the king and set off to the palace. When he was out of sight, the king turned to his men and laughed.

"We won't go hunting and now Mamad will lie to the queen," he cried.

At the palace, Mamad spoke to the queen.

"Maybe you should prepare a big feast for lunch, and maybe you shouldn't," said Mamad. "Maybe the king will come by noon, and maybe he won't."

"Tell me, will he come, or won't he?" asked the queen.

"I don't know whether he put his right foot on the other stirrup, or he put his left foot back on the ground after I left," replied Mamad.

Everybody waited for the king. He didn't arrive until the next day.

"The wise Mamad, who never lies, lied to you yesterday," boasted the king to the queen.

But the queen told him Mamad's exact words. The king realized that he couldn't fool Mamad. Indeed, a wise man never lies; he says only what he sees with his own eyes.

Rabbit's New Friend

Edward the rabbit loved night time best of all. He lived on a grassy hill next to a little forest. When the moon rose, he snuggled into his cosy tree-trunk den, opened his favorite book and read by the light of the stars. He loved listening to the owls hooting and the chirps of the grasshoppers.

The stories in his book were all about friends having adventures, and sometimes he wondered what that would be like.

"It might be fun to have a friend," he thought. But he never saw any other rabbits on the hill. So he just read his book and dreamed of playing games.

One night, Edward was reading his book as usual when something bright and sparkling landed next to him with a fizzing noise. It was followed by another . . . and another!

"What is it?" Edward cried. He looked up, and saw that some of the brightest stars were falling out of the sky. As he watched, the falling stars clustered together into the shape of a rabbit.

"Hello," said the star rabbit. "Want to play?"

Edward hopped out of his den. "Yes please!" he exclaimed.

What a night! The two rabbits played every game they could think of. They ran and chased and dug. They bounced and hopped and giggled. They ate all the carrots that Edward had stored in his den.

"I never knew it could be so much fun to have a friend," said Edward. "What shall we play next?"

"Hide-and-seek," said the star rabbit, and his eyes sparkled with mischief. "I'll hide."

Edward covered his eyes and counted to ten. When he looked, the star rabbit was nowhere to be seen. "Coming, ready or not!" Edward called. He searched through the long grass, behind tree trunks, and inside fallen logs, but there was no star rabbit.

Then he remembered his little den. He peered inside and saw a white, tufty tail.

"Found you!" he cried in delight.

The rabbit quickly hopped out of the den, but it wasn't the star rabbit. It was a white rabbit, and she was shivering.

"I got lost and I needed somewhere to rest," said the white rabbit. "My name is Sylvie."

"Would you like to play hide-and-seek, and meet my friend the star rabbit?" said Edward.

"I'd love to play hide-and-seek," said Sylvie, grinning. "And I've already met your friend. He showed me the way to your den."

She pointed up into the sky, and Edward gasped. The star rabbit had gone back to where he came from. The shape of a giant rabbit was shining in the sky.

Edward lay down on the
grass and Sylvie hopped over
and lay next to him. He told
Sylvie all about his games
and adventures with the star
rabbit. And as he looked up
into the night sky, he thought
he saw the star rabbit's eyes
give a mischievous twinkle.

"I hope you'll stay," said
Edward. "Now I know how
much fun it is to have a friend
to play with."

Sylvie nodded. "I've been
looking for a friend too,"
she said. "I'd love to stay."

And as the sun rose and the
stars disappeared, Edward and
his new friend Sylvie fell fast
asleep, hand in hand.

Kind Crane

Crane worked hard on the railroad, but the snooty express train ignored him. "I don't speak to lowly cranes," she said.

One day, the engineer was late. "I don't need him," said the express train. "I can drive myself." She pushed forward and set off toward the station. But she didn't notice a rock on the track. CRASH! She hit the rock and was knocked onto her side, with her wheels spinning. "Help!" she cried.

Crane bent down toward her. He used his hook and chain to gently lift her back onto her wheels. Then he knocked the rock from the track and pulled her back into position.

"Thank you," said the express. "But why are you helping me?"

"I think it's important to be kind," said Crane. The express felt bad. She knew that she hadn't been kind.

"I'm very sorry," she said. "From now on, we're a team!"

The Lonely Monster

People came from all over the world to see if they could spot the gigantic Lake Coco Monster. Then one day, a boy named Frankie was sitting by the lake when he heard a splash. He stayed very still, and he saw a monster creep out of the water.

"Wow!" said Frankie. "You're no bigger than a kitten!"

The monster jumped. "Oh please don't tell anyone you've seen me," it begged, trembling. "They'll be disappointed and they'll stop visiting the lake. I'll be lonelier than ever."

But Frankie knew better. "They'll love you!" he said. He showed the little monster how to play catch, and hide-and-seek. He brought his friends to meet it too, and soon the whole town knew what a perfect little monster was living in the lake. They had more visitors than ever, and the little monster was never lonely again. And as for the Lake Coco Monster ... the mystery still remains!

The Tortoise and the Hare

The tortoise and the hare were neighbors. Hare was always in a hurry, while Tortoise was happy to plod along, slowly and steadily.

One day, Tortoise was plodding along the road when Hare sped past him.

"You're so slow!" Hare called. "How do you ever get to where you're going?"

"I get everywhere I want to go!" Tortoise replied crossly. "I'll challenge you to a race."

"A race?" Hare laughed. "You don't stand a chance."

But they arranged a race for the next day, from an old oak tree all the way to the river, and asked Fox to judge it.

"On your marks ... get set ... go!" Fox shouted.

Hare sprinted ahead. Tortoise slowly set off.

After a few minutes, Hare could see the river ahead. He stopped. Tortoise was nowhere in sight.

"He won't be here for hours," he laughed. "I'll have a rest." Soon Hare dozed off.

Back along the path, Tortoise carried on, slow but steady.

After an hour, Hare woke up. He could just see Tortoise plodding toward him.

"He's so slow, he still won't be here for hours," Hare muttered, and went back to sleep.

When Hare woke up again, it was late afternoon. He looked down the road, but couldn't see Tortoise anywhere.

"I'll quickly finish the race, so I can go home," Hare sighed, bored with the race now.

Tortoise was waiting for him by the river.

"I've been here for hours!" cried Tortoise. "You are so slow!"

Hare tried to explain, but Tortoise and Fox wouldn't listen.

"But I'm faster!" Hare complained.

"The rules were simple," Fox said. "Tortoise won."

"The race was to get here first," Tortoise smiled, "not to run fastest. Slow and steady wins the race!"

Daddy

Bring Daddy home
With a fiddle and a drum,
A pocket full of spices,
An apple and a plum.

Clap Hands

Clap hands for Daddy coming
Down the wagon way,
With a pocketful of money,
And a cartload of hay.

Did You See My Wife?

Did you see my wife, did you see, did you see,
Did you see my wife looking for me?
She wears a straw bonnet, with white
ribbons on it,
And dimity petticoats over her knee.

My Aunt

I'm glad I've got an aunt,
She really is a winner.
She takes me out to feed the ducks,
And then she makes me dinner.

There Was an Old Man
With a Beard

There was an old man with a beard,
Who said, "It is just as I feared!—
Two owls and a hen, four larks, and a wren
Have all built their nests in my beard!"

My Mommy's Maid

Dingty diddlety,
My mommy's maid,
She stole oranges,
I am afraid;
Some in her pocket,
Some in her sleeve,
She stole oranges,
I do believe.

The Wolf and the Seven Young Kids

An old mother goat lived in a cottage with her seven little kids. One day she went out and left them alone, warning them the wolf might come, and that they must not let him in.

"Don't let that rascal trick you," she said. "He has a gruff old voice and his paws are as black as coal. That is how you will recognize him."

Sure enough, not long after the mother goat had left, there was a knock, knock, knock! at the door.

"Let me in," said a gruff old voice.

"We know it's you, wolf," said the kids. "You have such a gruff old voice."

So the wolf went away and ate some chalk to soften his voice. Then he went back to the goats' house and knocked on the door.

"Let me in," he said with his smooth, chalky voice. But the seven young kids noticed his black paws poking through a crack in the bottom of the door. "We know it's you, wolf," said the kids. "Your paws are as black as coal."

So the wolf went away and covered his paws with white flour. Then he went back to the goats' house and knocked on the door.

"Let me in," he said. His voice was not gruff and his paws were

not black, so the seven young kids opened the door and let him in.

In one huge gulp, the wolf ate six of the young kids, but the seventh one hid in a cupboard.

When the mother goat returned home, the seventh kid ran out from the cupboard and told her all about the wolf.

"Oh, my poor babies!" cried the mother goat. "We must go and find that wicked wolf." And they set off to look for him.

They found the old rascal sleeping beneath a tree. The mother goat carefully cut open the wolf's big fat stomach with a snip, snip, snip! Six young kids hopped out alive and well!

Then she picked up six stones and put them in the wolf's stomach before sewing it back up again.

The wolf woke up feeling thirsty and went to get some water. But the weight of the stones made him fall down the well, and he landed in the water with a SPLASH! And the wolf with the gruff old voice and paws as black as coal was never seen again.

The Swineherd

Not all princes live in gleaming palaces. Some have small kingdoms, few treasures, and only a crumbling castle to call their home. Once upon a time there was just such a prince. He was kind, bright, and handsome, and despite his noble birth, he had always been poor.

Soon the time came when the prince felt he was ready to marry. He didn't have great riches to offer a princess, but he was very well liked and there was a line of young ladies keen to accept his hand in marriage. But the prince had set his sights on the emperor's daughter. She was said to be very beautiful.

The prince decided to send the princess some gifts to prove his love for her. He chose the most precious things that he had: a beautiful rose from the tree that grew over his father's grave, and a divine song from his friend, a tiny nightingale, who lived in the castle garden.

The prince didn't know that the emperor's daughter was actually a spoiled and ungrateful girl. When she received the gifts, she threw the rose to the ground in a temper because it wasn't made of gold, and she sent the nightingale away when she saw that it was a dull brown color and not a jewel-encrusted clockwork bird.

But the prince was not ready to give up yet. He thought that if he was able to meet the princess in person, he could win her heart. Disguised as a poor farmhand, the prince went to the palace to ask for a job. The emperor needed someone to look after his pigs, so the prince accepted the job as his swineherd.

The prince had brought with him a special silver kettle, which had tiny bells on it. When the kettle boiled, the bells played a wonderful melody. He was boiling this kettle one day, when the princess and her ladies-in-waiting came over to his shed by the pigsties.

"This music is divine. I must have that kettle!" she cried rudely. "How much will you take for it?"

"It will cost you one hundred kisses," said the prince.

The princess looked at him in disgust. He was covered in mud and smelled bad, but she desperately wanted the kettle, so she agreed. She was just about to deliver the last kiss when her father suddenly appeared.

"What a disgrace!" he shouted, and threw them both out of the palace gates.

Outside, the prince revealed who he really was. The princess dropped down into a curtsey.

"Oh poor me! Your Highness, what shall I do?"

"You mocked my gifts from the heart, but you would kiss a swineherd for the sake of a kettle!" said the prince. "Take it. I will have nothing more to do with you."

334

The prince set off home. The princess gazed sadly after him. She was no longer wealthy, and all she had now was a musical kettle!

The Fox and the Tiger

One day a fox was walking through the forest when he met a tiger. The fox was afraid, but he said, "My dear sir, you must not think that you are the only king of the beasts!"

The tiger bared his teeth, but the fox bravely continued. "Your courage does not compare with mine. Walk behind me and I will show you. If no one is scared of me, then you may eat me up at once!"

The tiger decided to play along with the fox. As they walked through the forest, every animal that saw them ran away.

"You see!" the fox cried triumphantly. "All those animals saw me and ran away before they even caught sight of you!"

The tiger took one look at the fox and ran away himself! He had seen how terrified the other animals were, but he did not realize that it was him, and not the fox, they were really afraid of!

The Lion's Bad Breath

Lion was in a bad mood. Just that morning his wife had told him his breath smelled. He pretended he didn't care, but secretly he was worried, so he summoned three of his advisors - Sheep, Wolf, and Fox.

"Tell me, Sheep," growled Lion, "does my breath smell?"

The Sheep thought Lion wanted to know the truth, so she said, "Your Majesty, your breath smells terrible."

Lion was so angry he sent the poor sheep away forever! Then he asked Wolf, "Do you think my breath smells?"

"Your Majesty!" the trembling Wolf cried, "Your breath smells as sweet as the flowers in spring, as fresh as ..."

"Liar!" roared Lion before Wolf could finish, and sent him off too.

"So, Fox, does my breath smell?" said Lion menacingly.

Thinking quickly, the frightened fox coughed and sneezed and blew her nose. In a hoarse voice, she croaked, "I am so sorry, Your Majesty. I have such a nasty cold that I cannot smell anything!"

And that is how clever fox kept her job.

The Frog Kingdom

Felipe the frog was sitting beside the river with his friends when he saw a purple lily pad.

"First frog on the pad rules!" he shouted as he leaped. But as soon as his feet touched the lily pad, it shot off down the river. Felipe held on tight as the lily pad pushed through the leaves of a willow tree hanging over the water. On the other side, the lily pad suddenly slowed and things seemed different. Frogs that Felipe didn't know were cheering and waving to him from the bank. The lily pad stopped and Felipe sprang off.

"Welcome to your kingdom," said a tall frog, putting a crown on Felipe's head. "Three cheers for the king!"

Felipe looked around in amazement as the crowd led him through the watery streets of a city, filled with frogs' houses. Everyone came out to wave and bow. Felipe's palace was at the center, filled with velvety lily pads and cool, bubbling ponds.

"Your wish is our command!" said a frog in red uniform.

"Then I wish for a grand party," said Felipe. "Everyone in the kingdom is invited!"

The streets were filled with ribbons and balloons. Sweets were scattered from rooftops and sparkling water flowed from the fountains. Music filled the air and King Felipe danced with everyone. He was dancing beside the river when his foot slipped and he fell onto the purple lily pad. At once, it began to float back up the river.

"I don't want to go!" Felipe cried as the lily pad pushed back through the willow leaves.

His friends were waiting on the riverbank.

"I'm a king!" Felipe cried. "I rule the Frog Kingdom!"

His friends laughed, but Felipe knew that he hadn't been dreaming. He was still wearing his crown!

Bunny Loves to Learn

One morning, Buster Bunny and his best friends Sam the squirrel, Max the mouse, and Francine the frog arrived at school.

"What's in those boxes, Miss?" asked Buster.

"Costumes!" said Miss Nibbler. "Today you're going to dress up as people who lived a long time ago. I want you to make something from the time when they lived, and tell us all about it!"

"I'm going to find out about Vikings," said Buster.

"I want to be a knight," said Sam. "They have amazing helmets!"

"I think I'll be a princess!" cried Francine.

"I can't decide what to find out about," said Max.

"Why don't you dress up as an Egyptian ruler?" said Buster, taking a book from the shelf. "They were called pharaohs."

But the pharaoh's crown was missing from the box.

"I don't want to be a king without a crown!" said Max.

Just then he noticed a poster on the classroom wall.

"I want to be an Egyptian mummy!" he said. "They're so cool!"

He rummaged in the costume box.

"Drat," he said. "There's no mummy costume."

"I've got a knight's sword and helmet," said Sam. "I'm going to make a shield to go with them."

"I'm building a model of a Viking ship," said Buster.

"And I'm making a palace for a princess," said Francine.

Soon Buster, Sam, and Francine were busy making things. But Max still didn't know what to make.

"I really want to dress as a mummy," he grumbled.

"What else do you know about Egyptians?" asked Buster.

"I know they built big pyramids," said Max.

"Why don't you build one of those?" suggested Buster.

Max found some cardboard and tried to make a pyramid.

"Oh dear," he said. "This is trickier than I thought."

Francine showed him how to look up pyramids on the computer.

"Ah, now I see," said Max. "A pyramid has four sides, not three. And each side is exactly the same size."

Max finished his pyramid proudly,
but he still didn't know what to wear.

"Ouch!" said Buster suddenly. "I just got a paper cut!"

"It's only a small one," said Miss Nibbler. "But you'd better ask the school nurse for a bandage."

"That gives me an idea!" said Buster. He whispered in Max's ear.

"Great!" laughed Max. "Please don't be long!"

When it was time to present to the class, the friends took it in turns to show what they had made.

"I'm a knight," said Sam. "My shield protected me in battle. It was brightly painted so that my friends could recognize me when my helmet was shut!"

"I'm a princess," said Francine. "I lived in a palace. I wore long silky dresses and tall pointy hats. And I often got to boss around all the knights!"

Buster, back from the nurse, showed the class his Viking ship. "I'm a Viking," he said. "I loved to sail in a very fast ship called a longship. It had a dragon's head carved on the front to scare my enemies!"

"Thanks, Buster," said Miss Nibbler. "Now it's Max's turn."

"Egyptians lived a very, very long time ago," said Max's voice. But he was nowhere to be seen …

"They built amazing pyramids," the voice went on. "The pyramids were taller than ten houses on top of each other! Nobody lived in them, except for—MUMMIES! RAAAAH!"

And Max leaped out of the pyramid.

"So that's where you were hiding!" cried Francine.

"Where did you get that great mummy costume?" asked Sam. "I thought there wasn't one."

"I borrowed the bandages from the school nurse," said Max. "It was Buster's idea."

"Clever thinking, Buster!" said Miss Nibbler. "And well done to everybody. Your costumes look amazing and you've all learned some really interesting things. What a wonderful show and tell!"

Little Tommy Tucker

Little Tommy Tucker sings for his supper.
What shall we give him?
Brown bread and butter.
How shall he cut it without a knife?
How can he marry without a wife?

A Girl Named Mag

There was a girl named Mag with feet so large
That people cried, "They're as big as a barge!"
She wished for little feet, small and round,
But when she got them, she kept falling down.

Good Night

Good night, God bless you,
Go to bed and undress you.
Good night, sweet repose,
Half the bed and all the clothes.

When Jacky's a Good Boy

When Jacky's a very good boy,
He shall have cakes and a custard;
But when he does nothing but cry,
He shall have nothing but mustard

The Priest

The little priest of Felton,
The little priest of Felton,
He killed a mouse within his house,
And nobody there to help him.

My Shadow

I have a little shadow that goes in and out with me,
And what can be the use of him is more than I can see.
He is very, very like me from the heels up to the head;
And I see him jump before me, when I jump into my bed.

One morning, very early, before the sun was up,
I rose and found the shining dew on every buttercup;
But my lazy little shadow, like an errant sleepyhead,
Had stayed at home behind me and was fast asleep in bed.

The Fox and the Goat

One hot day, a thirsty fox was searching for something to drink. At last he found a well in a farmyard. He stuck his nose over the edge, but the water was too far down. Very carefully, he balanced on the side, trying to reach the cool, clear water. But though his nose was so close that he could smell it, he still couldn't quite reach the water.

The fox made one last try, stretching out his tongue with all his might. SPLASH! He toppled right in.

The sides of the well were so slippery that when the fox tried to climb out, he just kept sliding back down. He was stuck!

After a while, a goat came by looking for a drink. He was surprised to see the fox in the water.

"What on earth are you doing down there?" he asked.

"Just cooling down," replied the fox. "The water in this well is the best for miles around. Why don't you jump in and try it."

The goat was very hot and thirsty, and the water did look very refreshing, so he jumped in to join the fox.

"You're right!" said the goat, taking a long drink and relaxing in the water. "It's lovely and cool down here."

Soon the goat decided that it was time to go on his way.

"How do we get out?" he asked.

"That is a bit of a problem," the fox admitted.

"But I've got an idea. If you stick your legs out, you can wedge yourself in the well. Then I can climb on your back and jump out."

"That's all very well, but what about me?" the goat bleated.

"Once I've climbed out, I can help you get out," the fox explained.

So the goat wedged himself against the walls of the well and the fox clambered onto his back and leaped out.

"Thank you," laughed the fox, as he turned to leave.

"Hold on! What about me? How am I going to get out?" cried the goat.

"You should have thought about that before you jumped in," replied the sly fox, and off he ran.

And the moral of this story is: Always look before you leap.

Hansel and Gretel

Once upon a time, there were two children named Hansel and Gretel. They lived in a small cottage at the edge of the forest with their father, a poor woodcutter, and their stepmother.

One evening, the family had nothing left to eat but a few crusts of bread. Hansel and Gretel went to bed hungry. As they lay in their beds, they heard their parents talking.

"There are too many mouths to feed," said their stepmother. "We must take the children into the thickest part of the forest and leave them there."

"Never!" cried their father.

But the next morning, Hansel and Gretel's stepmother woke them early.

"Get up!" she ordered. "We're going into the forest to chop wood."

She handed them each a crust of bread for their lunch.

With a heavy heart, the woodcutter led his children into the forest. As they walked along, Hansel secretly dropped a trail of breadcrumbs along the path.

When they reached the middle of the forest, the woodcutter said, "Wait here. We'll return at sunset."

Hansel and Gretel waited all day, but their father and stepmother didn't come back. Soon, it was dark among the thick trees and Gretel was frightened.

"Don't worry," said Hansel, cuddling his sister. "We'll follow the trail of breadcrumbs I dropped along the path. They will lead us home."

But when the moon came up, they couldn't see any crumbs.

"Oh, no! The birds must have eaten them all!" whispered Hansel.

Hansel and Gretel curled up under a tree and fell fast asleep.

The next morning, they wandered through the forest until they came to a little cottage made of gingerbread and candies!

The children were so hungry they picked candies off the house and crammed them into their mouths.

Just then, the door opened and an old woman hobbled out.

"Come in, children," she said, smiling. "I've got plenty more food in here."

The old woman fed them well and then put them to bed. But Hansel and Gretel didn't know that the old woman was actually a wicked witch who liked to eat children!

When Hansel and Gretel woke up, the witch grabbed Hansel and locked him in a cage. She set Gretel to work cooking huge meals to fatten up Hansel.

The weeks went by and every morning the witch went up to the cage, asking Hansel to hold out his finger.

"I want to feel if you are fat enough to eat," she said.

Hansel, being a smart boy, held out an old chicken bone instead. The witch's eyesight was so bad that she thought the bone was Hansel's finger.

One day, the witch got tired of waiting for the boy to get fatter and decided to cook him right away.

Grabbing Gretel's arm, she said, "Go and check if the oven is hot enough." And she pushed Gretel toward the open oven door. Grinning horribly, she licked her cracked lips. She was planning to eat Gretel too, and couldn't wait for her delicious meal.

"I'm too big to fit in there," said Gretel, guessing the witch's wicked plan.

"You silly girl," cackled the witch. "Even I could fit in there." And she stuck her head inside. With a great big shove, Gretel pushed the witch into the oven and slammed the door shut.

"Hansel, the witch is dead!" cried Gretel, unlocking her brother's cage.

As the children made their way out of the house, they found chests crammed with gold and sparkling jewels. They filled their pockets and set off home.

Their father was overjoyed to see them. He told them that their stepmother had died while they were gone so they had nothing to fear any more. Hansel and Gretel showed their father the treasure.

"We will never go hungry again!" he cried.

And they all lived happily ever after.

I Love You, Grandpa

Little Bear and Grandpa were walking by the river when Little Bear spotted a fish darting through the water.

"Quick, Grandpa!" he yelled. He rushed into the river, caught the fish, and held it up proudly for Grandpa to see.

Grandpa smiled. "My legs were once strong and speedy like yours," he said. "But now I've found an easier way to catch a meal."

"Really, Grandpa?" asked Little Bear. "What's that?"

"Well," replied Grandpa, "I'm craftier now. I stand here at the rapids and I wait until the fish jump out of the water ... straight into my mouth."

"Wow!" said Little Bear. "I love you, Grandpa. You're so clever!"

Just then, Eagle swooped down. The beat of his wings ruffled the bears' fur. They saw his sharp claws.

Little Bear ran straight up a tree. Grandpa smiled.

"I can remember when I could climb as well as you," he said. "But now I don't need to run away."

"Really, Grandpa?" asked Little Bear. "What do you do?"

"Well," replied Grandpa, "I'm bolder now." When Eagle swooped again, Grandpa barked in his deep, gruff voice. He roared, and Eagle swerved away over the mountains.

"I love you, Grandpa," said Little Bear. "You're so brave!"

They walked on until they came across a slope where the earth was softer and deeper.

"Watch me, Grandpa!" called Little Bear. "I can dig myself a really good hollow to sleep in through the winter."

Grandpa smiled. "I can remember when I could dig as well as you," he sighed. "But now I know a better way to find a hollow."

"Really, Grandpa?" frowned Little Bear. "But where do you spend the winter?"

"Well," replied Grandpa, "I'm wiser now. All I need to do is to find a hollow tree. Follow me." And he led Little Bear to a huge tree.

In the middle of its massive trunk was a snug hollow.

"I love you, Grandpa," said Little Bear. "You know so much. Will I ever be as crafty, brave and wise as you?"

"Of course you will!" replied Grandpa. He hugged Little Bear close. "I love you too, Little Bear."

The Crow and the Pitcher

One hot summer day, when there had been no rain for months and all the ponds and rivers had dried up, a thirsty crow was searching for a drink. At last he spotted a pitcher of cool water in a garden, and flew down to take a drink. But when he put his head into the neck of the pitcher, it was only half full, and the crow could not reach the water.

Now, the crow was a smart bird, so he came up with a plan—he would break the neck of the pitcher, then reach down to the water below.

Tap! Tap! Tap! The crow pecked the pitcher with his sharp beak again and again, but it was so hard and strong, he couldn't make even the tiniest crack.

The crow did not give up easily, so he thought of another plan. He would tip the pitcher over. The bird pushed and pushed as hard as he could, but the pitcher was very heavy, and it would not move at all.

The poor crow knew that if he did not get a drink soon he would die of thirst. He had to find some way of getting to the water in the pitcher! As he looked around, wondering what to do, he saw some pebbles on the path, and he had an idea.

He picked up a pebble in his beak and dropped it into the pitcher. The water level rose a little. The bird got another pebble and dropped it in. The water rose a little more. The crow worked very hard, dropping more and more pebbles into the pitcher until the water was almost at the top.

At last the bird was able to reach the water—and he drank and drank until he could drink no more. His clever idea had saved his life.

And the moral of the story is: Little by little does the trick.

Counting Stars

Tomorrow was Little Panda's first day at school, and she was very excited. Daddy tucked her up in bed, but she was too wide awake to close her eyes.

"I wonder what new friends I'll meet?" she said. "I can't wait to find my desk and meet my teacher. School is going to be so much fun!"

Daddy tried to make Little Panda feel sleepy. He read stories, he sang lullabies, and he stroked her soft fur, but she was still wide awake.

"All right," he said. "Whatever you do, don't go to sleep. You must stay awake until you have counted every single star in the sky."

The sky was crowded with twinkling stars. Little Panda started to count them.

"One ... two ... three ... four ..."

Before she even reached number ten, Little Panda's eyelids had drooped and she'd fallen fast asleep. And what did she dream about? Her first day at school, of course!

Lion's First Day

It was clumsy Lion's first day at Miss Giraffe's Savannah School. True to his nature, he arrived late, skidded into the classroom, tripped over his paws, and landed upside down in his chair.

Miss Giraffe tilted her head and smiled kindly at Lion.

"What an amazing acrobat you are!" she said.

At lunchtime, Lion bumped into the table and knocked all the food over. Then he spilled his drink and slipped across the floor.

"What wonderful clown skills you have!" said Miss Giraffe.

At recess, Lion tripped over and knocked some balls off a shelf, catching three with his paws and one on the tip of his tail.

"What a fantastic juggler you'd make!" said Miss Giraffe.

That evening, Lion couldn't wait to tell his mother about his day.

"All this time I thought I was clumsy, but Miss Giraffe thinks I'm an acrobat!" he said. "And a clown and a juggler!"

His mother smiled.

"You can be a magician too, just make your dinner disappear!"

The Boy Who Cried Wolf

Once there was a boy named Peter who lived in a little village in the mountains with his parents, who were sheep farmers. It was Peter's job to watch over the flock and protect the sheep from wolves.

Every day, Peter sat on the mountainside watching the flock. It was very quiet with no one but sheep for company. No wolves ever came to eat the sheep.

"Oh, I wish something exciting would happen," groaned Peter. "I'm so bored!"

Finally, one day, Peter couldn't stand it any more. He started shouting at the top of his voice:

"WOLF! HELP! WOLF!"

Down in the village, a man heard Peter's cries.

"Quick!" he shouted. "There's a wolf attacking the sheep."

The villagers grabbed their axes, forks, and shovels and ran up the mountain to where Peter was shepherding his flock.

When they got there, the sheep were grazing peacefully.

"Where's the wolf?" one of the villagers cried.

Peter roared with laughter. "There's no wolf. I was just playing!"

The villagers were very angry. "You mustn't cry wolf when there isn't one," they said.

That night Peter got a telling-off from his mother and was sent to bed without any supper.

For a while after this, Peter managed to behave himself, and the villagers soon forgot about his trick.

Then one day, Peter was bored again. Laughing, he picked up some sticks and started banging them hard together. Then at the top of his voice, he shouted, "WOLF! Help! WOLF! There's a big wolf eating the sheep!"

Down in the village, a crowd of people started gathering when they heard the loud banging and shouting.

"It's Peter," someone cried. "Quick, there must be a wolf on the prowl."

Once again, the villagers grabbed their axes, forks, and shovels. They ran up the mountain to chase away the wolf and save poor Peter and his sheep.

And once again, when they got there, the sheep were grazing peacefully.

"Peter, what's happened?" shouted one man angrily.

"There's no wolf," laughed Peter. "I was only playing."

"You shouldn't do that," said another man. "It's not good to lie."

That night, Peter got an even bigger telling-off from his mother and once again had to go to bed without any supper.

Peter decided that he would really try and behave himself from now on, and soon the incident was forgotten.

A few weeks later, while Peter stood counting the sheep to pass the time, he noticed that some of them were bleating nervously.

He climbed up a tree to see what was upsetting them.

To his horror, he saw a big wolf creeping through the grass toward the flock.

Shaking with fear he started screaming, "WOLF! Help! WOLF! Please hurry, there's a big wolf about to eat the sheep!"

A few people down in the village heard his cries for help, but they carried on about their business as usual.

"It's only Peter playing another trick," they said to each other. "Does he think he can fool us again?"

And so nobody went to Peter's rescue.

By nightfall, when Peter hadn't returned, his parents became concerned. Peter never missed his supper—something bad must have happened.

The villagers hurried up the mountain, carrying flaming torches to light their way.

A terrible sight met their eyes. All the sheep were gone! There really had been a wolf this time.

Peter was still in the tree, shaking and crying.

"I cried out wolf! Why didn't you come?" he wept.

"Nobody believes a liar, even when he's speaking the truth," said Peter's father, helping him climb out of the tree. Peter hung on to his father all the way home. He never wanted to see another wolf ever again.

And Peter finally really learned his lesson. He never told a lie again, and he always got to eat his dinner.

The Three Billy Goats Gruff

Long ago, there were three brothers—a little goat, a medium-sized goat, and a big goat.

The brothers lived in a field of short, dry grass beside a river.

On the other side of the river, over a bridge, was a huge meadow with long, juicy grass.

The goats longed to taste the juicy grass, but the bridge was guarded by a horrible, ugly troll.

One day, the little Billy Goat Gruff plucked up his courage and trotted over the bridge.

TRIP TRAP, TRIP TRAP went his feet.

"Who's that TRIP TRAPPING over my bridge?" cried the troll, leaping in front of the little goat. "I will eat you!"

"Please don't!" cried the little goat.

"Wait for my brother—he is much bigger and tastier than me."

"All right," said the greedy troll, and he let the little goat cross.

Later that day, the medium-sized goat saw his little brother munching juicy grass on the other side, and wanted to eat it, too.

So he set off, TRIP TRAP, TRIP TRAP, across the bridge.

"Who's that TRIP TRAPPING over my bridge?" cried the troll again. "I will eat you!"

"Please don't!" cried the medium-sized goat. "Wait for my brother—he is much bigger and tastier than me."

The greedy troll licked his lips, and let the medium-sized Billy Goat Gruff cross the bridge.

At last it was the big Billy Goat Gruff's turn to cross the bridge. TRIP TRAP, TRIP TRAP went his hooves on the wooden bridge.

"Who's that TRIP TRAPPING over my bridge?" bellowed the troll, drooling at the sight of the big goat. "I will eat you!"

But the big Billy Goat Gruff was not afraid of the ugly troll.

"You can't eat me!" shouted the big Billy Goat Gruff. He lowered his head, stamped his hooves, and tossed the troll into the river with his great big billy goat horns.

Then the biggest goat went TRIP TRAP, TRIP TRAP over the bridge to join his brothers, and the horrible troll never bothered them again!

Baby in a Cradle

The baby in the cradle
Goes rock-a-rock-a-rock.
The clock on the dresser
Goes tick-a-tick-a-tock.
The rain on the window
Goes tap-a-tap-a-tap,
But here comes the sun,
So we clap-a-clap-a-clap!

Rock-A-Bye, Baby

Rock-a-bye, baby, on the tree top,
When the wind blows, the cradle will rock.
When the bough breaks, the cradle will fall,
Down will come baby, cradle and all.

I See the Moon

I see the moon and the moon sees me.
God bless the moon and God bless me.

Little Fred

When little Fred went to bed,
He always said his prayers,
He kissed Mom, and then Papa,
And straightaway went upstairs.

Go to Bed, Tom

Go to bed, Tom,
Go to bed, Tom,
Tired or not, Tom,
Go to bed, Tom.

Bend and Stretch

Bend and stretch, reach for the stars.
There goes Jupiter, here comes Mars.
Bend and stretch, reach for the sky.
Stand on tip-e-toe, oh! So high!

Mowgli and Baloo's Lessons

Baloo, the big brown bear, was teaching Mowgli the Law of the Jungle. There was so much to learn that Mowgli sometimes got things wrong and Baloo would tell him off with a gentle cuff around the ears.

Mowgli had just been in trouble again, and he stormed off and hid in the trees.

"Don't be so hard on him, my old friend," said Bagheera, the black panther, who had been watching the lesson from the cover of the long grass.

"He needs to learn, so he doesn't come to harm," grumbled Baloo. "At the moment I'm teaching him the Master Words of the Jungle, which will protect him from all the jungle creatures. Come, little man cub, stop sulking, and show Bagheera what you know."

Mowgli slid down a tree trunk and pulled a face at Baloo.

"I'm only coming down for Bagheera," complained Mowgli. "The jungle has many tongues and I know them all." And he rattled off several of the jungle languages, happy to show off his language skills to Bagheera.

"One day I'll lead my own tribe, and we'll throw sticks and dirt at Baloo!" laughed Mowgli.

"Mowgli," growled Baloo. "You've been talking to the Monkey People. They're evil."

Sheepishly, Mowgli looked at Bagheera.

"It's true, man cub," said the wise panther. "They lie and cheat. They have no Law. Baloo is right, you must stay away from them."

Unbeknown to either Baloo or Bagheera, some of the Monkey People were hiding in the trees above. They waited until the three friends were asleep and then they grabbed Mowgli and swung him away through the treetops.

Mowgli was frightened. He knew that he had to get word back to his friends so they could rescue him. He saw Chil, the kite bird, circling above the trees and remembered Baloo's lessons. He called to the bird in his language.

369

"The Monkey People have kidnapped me and are taking me to their city. Tell Baloo and Bagheera."

Meanwhile, Baloo and Bagheera were running through the jungle looking for Mowgli. When they got Chil's message they headed for the ancient ruins which the Monkeys called their home. Before they got to the lost city, they came across Kaa, the python.

"What are you hunting?" hissed the snake.

"Monkey People, who have snatched Mowgli," explained Baloo.

"Ah, chattering, vain foolish things," sighed Kaa. "I'll help you."

At the ruined city, the Monkey People gathered around Mowgli.

"Teach us to be like man," they cried. "And we will be the wisest people in the jungle!"

Mowgli was wondering how he could escape, when Bagheera raced into the ruins, knocking down monkeys everywhere. But there were too many for the brave panther to fend off.

"Roll into the water tank," cried Mowgli. "They won't follow you there."

Bagheera lunged into the water tank just as Baloo arrived and took up the fight. Then Kaa pounced. He was everything the monkeys feared. They scattered with cries of "It's Kaa, run, run!"

Mowgli was free from the clutches of the terrible Monkey People.

"Little man, I'm so proud of you that you remembered the Master Words of the Jungle," cried Baloo, giving Mowgli a huge bear hug.

After that day, Mowgli always tried his best to remember everything Baloo taught him.

Chicken Little

One day, an acorn fell on Chicken Little's head, then rolled away.

"Oh, my," clucked Chicken Little, panicked. "THE SKY IS FALLING!"

"Cluck-a-cluck-cluck!" shrieked Henny Penny. "We must tell the king!"

So they flapped down the road, and met Cocky Locky.

"Where are you going in such a hurry?" he asked.

"THE SKY IS FALLING!" cried Chicken Little. "We're off to tell the king!"

"Cock-a-doodle-doo," crowed Cocky Locky. "I'll come, too!"

So Chicken Little, Henny Penny, and Cocky Locky rushed off to tell the king. Soon they met Ducky Lucky.

"Why are you flapping so?" she asked.

"THE SKY IS FALLING!" cried Chicken Little. "We're off to tell the king!"

"C-can I c-c-come?" quacked Ducky Lucky nervously.

So Chicken Little, Henny Penny, Cocky Locky, and Ducky Lucky rushed off to tell the king.

Soon they met Drakey Lakey.

"What's all this fuss?" he asked.

"THE SKY IS FALLING!" cried Chicken Little. "We're off to tell the king!"

"I'll join you," squawked Drakey Lakey.

So Chicken Little, Henny Penny, Cocky Locky, Ducky Lucky, and Drakey Lakey rushed off to tell the king.

Soon they met Goosey Loosey and Turkey Lurkey.

"What's ruffled your feathers?" Goosey Loosey asked.

"THE SKY IS FALLING!" cried Chicken Little. "We're off to tell the king!"

"Goodness," gobbled Turkey Lurkey.

"We'll come!" honked Goosey Loosey.

So Chicken Little, Henny Penny, Cocky Locky, Ducky Lucky, Drakey Lakey, Goosey Loosey, and Turkey Lurkey rushed off to tell the king.

Soon they met Foxy Loxy.

"Hello!" he said. "Where are you all going?"

"THE SKY IS FALLING!" cried Chicken Little. "We're off to tell the king!"

Foxy Loxy grinned slyly. "I know a shortcut. Follow me."

So they did … right into Foxy Loxy's den!

"RUN!" cried Chicken Little.

And the seven birds ran home, flapping and flurrying, as fast as they could.

And they never did get to tell the king about the sky falling.

Trixie the Troll

Long ago, after a wicked old troll had been caught bullying billy goats once too often, trolls from every corner of the globe were banished to a small land of gray skies and swirling mists at the bottom of the world.

At first, the trolls liked their new home. They were free to spend their days picking their enormous noses and making rude noises without the tiresome task of scaring humans and goats.

There was only problem. Trolls had always lived alone under bridges and in caves. Many of them had never even met another troll! But in their small land, where there was barely space to scratch, their odors mingled to make one unbearable STINK!

For the first time they noticed that their fur was caked in food, their claws were filthy, and their breath was eye-wateringly horrific.

One shy little troll, called Trixie, felt so ashamed of her smell, she summoned all her courage and spoke up.

"Perhaps we should wash," she murmered.

The other trolls looked at her in disbelief. But Trixie was determined. She walked down to the river and gingerly dipped a slimy toe in the river, then waded in up to her knees and finally plunged into the current. It felt wonderfully cool and refreshing! As she laughed and splashed and a scrubbed, a few curious trolls gathered on the riverbank to watch. Before long they were all wallowing in the water, and by the time they had finished they smelt as fresh as mountain dew!

That was the start of a new way of living.

Now trolls are a clean bunch. They spend their days washing in the river, combing their silky fur, brushing their pearly fangs and clipping their spotlessy clean claws. But they still enjoy some of their old pastimes, like making rude noises, shouting silly things out loudly, picking their enormous noses, and proudly flicking their boogers at their friends!

Twinkle, Twinkle, Little Star

Twinkle, twinkle, little star,
How I wonder what you are!
Up above the world so high,
Like a diamond in the sky.

When the blazing sun is gone,
When he nothing shines upon,
Then you show your little light,
Twinkle, twinkle, all the night.

Bed in Summer

In winter I get up at night,
And dress by yellow candlelight.
In summer, quite the other way,
I have to go to bed by day.

Golden Slumbers

Golden slumbers kiss your eyes,
Smiles await you when you rise.
Sleep, pretty baby, do not cry,
And I will sing a lullaby.

Later that day, the fir tree found itself in a grand room, standing in a pot and covered in glittering decorations, presents, candies, and lights. It felt marvelous!

"I wonder how long I shall be on display like this?" it pondered happily. "All winter perhaps? Maybe all summer, too?"

But the very next day the children came and grabbed the presents and sweets from its branches. Then, the following morning, a man came and took down the lights and decorations, before throwing the little fir tree out into a yard, where it was cut into logs for the fire.

"If only I had enjoyed my time in the forest instead of wasting it," the fir tree sighed. "I should have treasured every moment."

The fir tree finally saw things clearly. As it melted into the fire, the little fir tree gave thanks for the beauty it had seen in its life.

Index

384